PACIFIC BEACH

A Jillian Bradley
Mystery

Book 5

NANCY JILL THAMES

Pacific Beach

Cover Design by LLewellen Designs:
www.lyndseylewellen.wordpress.com

Formatting by Libris in CAPS:
www.librisincaps.wordpress.com

Photo Credits:
Casual blond Zdenka Darula/Dreamstime.com
Night swimming pool against the palm Seqoya/Dreamstime.com
Moody beach Andyfox0co0uk/Dreamstime.com
Yorkie Copyright: Scorpp/shutterstock.com
Author Photo: Glamour Shots Barton Creek
Yorkshire terrier: "Romeo" Courtesy: Dan and Sara Olla

ISBN-13: 978-1466237780
ISBN-10: 1466237783
Category: *Fiction/Mystery Series/Women Sleuths/Cozy Mystery/Inspirational Fiction*

ACKNOWLEDGEMENTS

If it were not for my wonderful parents who hosted our family reunion in Pacific Beach, this book would have never been written. Thank you, Mom and Dad. I wish also to thank my incredible beta readers: Roxanne Day; LeAnn McConnell; Donna Montgomery; and Marie Thayamballi for their editorial contributions. A thank you is also in order for my longsuffering husband, Ted, for all his helpful input in writing this book. Finally, a huge thank you to the members of my family who allowed me to use their personae in the characters I created.

CONTENTS

Chapter 1   *The Nightmare*
Chapter 2   *The Arrival*
Chapter 3   *Lobby Drama*
Chapter 4   *Poolside*
Chapter 5   *Family Meeting*
Chapter 6   *Surprise Guest*
Chapter 7   *Photo Shoot*
Chapter 8   *Double Homicide*
Chapter 9   *Emergency Meeting*
Chapter 10   *Party Guests*
Chapter 11   *Errant Wife*
Chapter 12   *A Good Omen*
Chapter 13   *Kickball on the Beach*
Chapter 14   *Emily Woods*
Chapter 15   *Lee Sterling*
Chapter 16   *Alex Draper and Fancy*
Chapter 17   *The Pizza Guy*
Chapter 18   *Departures*
Chapter 19   *Night Meeting*
Chapter 20   *Another Homicide*
Chapter 21   *Disappearance*
Epilogue
Also by Nancy Jill Thames
ABOUT THE AUTHOR

1 The Nightmare

June 8 — San Diego, California

Caroline played innocently in her own front yard with her new puppy when the car struck her down. The golden-haired mutt had been rescued by her father before their neighbor could drop the defenseless dog off in the country to fend for itself.

Caroline named him Buddy.

The frisky pup gently licked the little girl's face as she hugged him. Wanting to pretend he was her baby, she coaxed Buddy to be still and struggled to put the pink doll dress over his head. Normal play for a five-year-old girl. Finally, she succeeded and giggled at how funny Buddy looked in the frilly doll dress.

Caroline's nine-year-old brother was in the driveway of their modest home. The boy stooped over the back tire of his bicycle and attached playing cards to the spokes with clothespins. He imagined the cards made the sound of a motorcycle like his uncle's 650.

The children's mother watched her daughter but needed to go inside the house to check on a cake in the oven. Her mind was burdened with how to pay the bills from her handy-man husband's meager paycheck. The afternoon was late, and it was almost time for him to come home from work.

Supper was almost ready, a meager meal of Hamburger Helper. But there would be cake. No matter how hard they struggled to merely survive, they remained a close-knit family.

And then the unthinkable happened. A late-model car came out of nowhere, speeding, swerving wildly.

Caroline's brother watched helplessly as the driver ran up over the curb and into their yard. Buddy scampered away in the pink doll dress, terrified, and Caroline sat frozen on the lawn, staring wide-eyed as the car came toward her.

The boy watched in horror as the car struck her small, defenseless body and tossed it further into the yard. He heard the tires squeal as the car raced off — the driver not even bothering to stop.

The boy, almost in shock, had enough presence of mind to notice the license plate. His parents had drilled both of their children with the importance of protective safety measures. Now the numbers were burned into his memory forever. He frantically ran to his sister and wondered how he was going to help her.

The frightened boy bent down and cradled her bloodied body in his arms. Angry and helpless, he vowed the maniac would be caught.

The mother, hearing screeching tires so close to her house, came outside, drying her hands on her apron, to see what was going on. She looked in the yard and found her son holding the lifeless body in his arms. She ran toward them, holding her head with her hands, and screamed at the terrible thing that had just happened.

The boy turned to her. "Call 911!"

That was the beginning of the nightmare — for the mother, for the father, and for the nine-year-old boy.

June 18 — Twelve Years Later

The nightmare culminated in a tragic double-homicide at the Pacific Terrace Hotel where I stayed. Before the ordeal, I remember feeling so happy. *The San Francisco Enterprise* had just published two great articles for my *Ask Jillian* gardening column, and I had time for a breather. I also looked forward to attending our family reunion.

My personal assistant, Cecilia Montoya, came with me to help take care of Teddy, my Yorkie companion. The three of us flew into San Diego International Airport two days before the tragedy occurred.

2 The Arrival

I looked out my window at beautiful San Diego Harbor below. Sailboats and dinghies of every size and color were moored on the deep blue Pacific.

San Diego is the second largest city in California and the ninth largest city in the United States. Pacific Beach is a laid-back surfer town with a lovely average temperature of seventy degrees. The dress is extremely casual, and flip flops reign as the most popular shoe choice.

San Diego has been called "the most exciting city in California," and I could understand why. For starters, there's Balboa Park, home of The San Diego Zoo, which features the finest collection of animals in the world. There are numerous theme parks, museums, and plenty of shopping opportunities. Seaport Village and the Gaslamp Quarter (filled with all kinds of restaurants and shops) are two favorites. The quaint Old Town Trolley is available to help navigate around.

As we prepared to land, I felt a small shiver of excitement run down my back at the thought of seeing my family again. I feel closer to my true identity at every Lovejoy family reunion. Last year there had been twenty of us. This year, we had twenty-one coming, including two new babies.

I suppose I should've included Teddy in the count. He's my Yorkie companion that travels with me wherever I go.

Of course, I took my personal assistant, Cecilia Chastain — I mean Montoya — along. I must remember she's married now.

I've known her for so long I always think of her as a young college girl working her way through school as a hotel housekeeper.

It's wonderful having someone to take charge of Teddy when I can't, not to mention the help she gives me with correspondence, research and anything else I can think of.

I know I'm a bit eccentric, but a Yorkie of mine was kidnapped years ago in Half Moon Bay and was quite traumatized from the ordeal. After that happened, I vowed never to leave my dog unattended in a hotel room again, so I pay Cecilia to accompany me when I travel.

She's intelligent and quite competent, but the best thing about Cecilia is she is such pleasant company for me.

I closed my computer and shut it down, having finally finished my article for this week's *Ask Jillian* gardening column. I'd written about one of my favorite perennials, penstemon — purple fountain grass. At least penstemon is a perennial unless a region has freezing temperatures. Then the poor plant doesn't have a chance.

The landing gear touched down, and I silently thanked the Lord for a safe trip. Teddy heaved a sigh indicating he was ready to come out from underneath the seat in front of me and get out of his travel carrier. He's so smart — he's figured out how to unzip it with his nose.

"Be patient for a few more minutes and I'll take you out, sweet doggie."

Cecilia stretched but didn't smile like she usually did.

"Everything okay, dear?"

She offered a small unconvincing smile.

"I'm okay. Just feeling a little blah."

"Wait until you smell the sea air. Maybe you'll feel better."

"I'm sure it's nothing, Jillian. Don't worry about me."

But I did worry about her. I had no one else to worry about, except for Teddy.

As we taxied to the gate, my thoughts turned to the reunion.

I can't wait! I can't wait! Such posts had been flying back and forth between my nieces, and with good reason.

Every year, the Lovejoy family gathers for the annual family reunion — a fun-filled time for four wonderful days with nothing to do but relax.

Rarely does anyone miss it, unless it's due to circumstances beyond their control, like my nephew-in-law, Kenny, serving in Afghanistan this year.

As a major incentive, Grandmother Lovejoy picks up the hotel tab for the married grandkids. Everyone else is on their own. Not many young couples with children can afford such luxury, so the grandchildren are quite appreciative.

Our family pretty much takes over the hotel, which is right on Pacific Beach, and we have been doing so as a tradition for more years than I can remember.

Other guests are in residence, of course, but we really only see our family. It's difficult to keep our happy reunion quiet since there's a great deal of laughter most of the time.

We haven't been kicked out yet, but we have been asked to quiet down on at least one occasion when we got a little out-of-hand down by the pool. It was after hours, and some of the other guests requested we be asked to converse a little quieter.

When this happens, we take our party to the Cayman Room, or the Lovejoy Bunker, as we lovingly refer to it. Not only are there plenty of tables and chairs to accommodate our group, but there is a fully-stocked kitchen as well. Games are pulled out, and we play until the kids need to be put down for the night or we older adults need to retire for the evening. Afterward, the younger adults get together and go out on the town for some lively fun.

All the females take pictures to record the events. Posts are up within the hour on Facebook. We can't wait for shopping, boogie boarding, going out for lunch and dinner, baseball games, visiting museums or theme parks, going to the movies, walks along the boardwalk, swimming, and last but not least — the hot tub.

The three of us exited the plane with me carrying Teddy since Cecilia felt blah. He would stay safe that way.

The airport was crowded, as usual, since San Diego is a major tourist destination. The long security lines reminded me to arrive early for the trip home.

We reached the baggage claim area, where I saw a gentleman in a black suit holding an iPad that read, "Jillian Bradley."

I waved, and the man came toward our small party.

He smiled. "I'll get your luggage."

Taking Teddy out of his cramped carrier and placing him in his roomier crate, we found a limo waiting for us in the airport parking lot.

Teddy's cage fit snugly in the back seat with Cecilia and me as we headed north to our destination. The driver made polite conversation. I was happy to oblige, answering his standard touristy questions.

I made the usual responses, but my thoughts were centered on the familiar route we were taking.

It was late Saturday morning, and traffic was light. We drove past the harbor, onto the freeway and out of downtown San Diego, until the driver exited on Garnet Avenue and traveled down the road toward Pacific Beach.

Teddy yipped as we passed a billboard advertising a Surf Dog competition that week.

A few moments later, I saw the familiar Mission Beach Arch, gateway to the boardwalk of Pacific Beach.

The driver made a right turn on Mission Street, which dead-ended at the boardwalk.

Another shiver of excitement ran down my back in anticipation as we approached the last turn. Only one more left turn onto Diamond Street. From there, it was just a half a block to the beach. We made a quick right and finally reached the guest parking lot of The Pacific Terrace Hotel. Tall palm trees, with their fronds swaying gently in the ocean breeze, towered in front of the hotel balconies, all of which had ocean views. Colorful flowers grew everywhere in the well-maintained landscape. I had known the head gardener here for years.

The Pacific Terrace Hotel is one of the classiest hotels in Pacific Beach. It has the only four-star diamond rating for a beachfront hotel. Right on the boardwalk, it's adjacent to the main hub for shops and restaurants only a short walk away.

This beautiful hotel is my home away from home. We've been coming here for the past ten years, not finding a place that could be any more perfectly suited to our needs.

I can travel back in time here, reliving my childhood as our family shares delightful memories of growing up together. My mother, Louise Lovejoy, acts shocked sometimes at the childhood antics we confess, formerly unbeknown to her.

Or were they?

All I know is we laugh a great deal when we're together — especially at this wonderful hotel.

I got out of the limo, held Teddy's crate, and heard the ocean's roar as it hurled white-crested waves onto the shore.

Teddy's nose twitched as he strained to smell the new environment.

I attached his red rhinestone-studded leash to his collar and placed him in his rather worn cheetah tote, where he'd be more comfortable.

It was slightly overcast as we arrived, but that was typical for Pacific Beach. The fog usually cleared by mid-morning.

I inhaled the cool sea air and listened to the roar of the ocean as some seagulls flew by, calling to each other as they passed overhead.

Teddy yipped at them from his tote and strained to smell their scent before they flew out of sight.

Our driver gathered the luggage and followed Cecilia and me into the hotel.

Emerald-encrusted dragons with ruby eyes guarded the entry doors of the lobby. Bamboo chairs upholstered in a tropical print gave a feeling of an island retreat. Hanging tapestries adorned the walls. Dark wooden shutters covered the windows.

Two life-sized bronze cranes stood next to large planters filled with bromeliads and prayer plants. Terra cotta floors added to the tropical feel of the room and hallways.

The lobby felt familiar. I was home.

The driver handed the luggage to a valet. I paid him. He tipped his hat, thanked me, and left through the open double doors.

I felt the warmth immediately from the terra cotta tile floors to the desk clerks, who glanced at us with smiles, welcoming us back to this familiar place.

At one end of the check-in counter stood a large clamshell which held ripe red apples. On the other end was a domed cake stand, holding freshly-baked chocolate chip cookies.

To resist the temptation, I turned to Teddy. He was husband and children to me. My husband died in the Vietnam War, and I was never able to have any children. Because I need to care for something in this world, something close and immediate, Teddy is the one I care for. Admittedly, I do get carried away at times lavishing affection on him.

Since Cecilia wasn't feeling well, I didn't ask her to take him for a walk like I usually would have due to my lack of stamina. He seemed content. Hopefully, Cecilia would feel better after getting some fresh air.

Before I approached the desk to check in, my sister Brooke saw me from the hallway corridor.

"Jillian! You made it! Hi, Cecilia. Hello, Teddy."

After hugs all around, Brooke took Teddy out of his tote and lavished him with more love. "Everyone's here except for Will and the girls. Chase is at the pool, of course. You know him."

I laughed. "Checking out the girls, I would imagine, at his age. How old is he now?"

"He's twenty. I can hardly believe it myself. He's doing well in the Marine Corps Reserve. Seems to like it."

"Excuse me," said Cecilia, "I think I'm a little tired from the trip." She walked over to a chair and sat down.

"I do hope she's not coming down with something," said Brooke. "Seems like at every reunion someone gets sick and shares it."

"I wouldn't worry," I said. "She just needs some fresh air and some fish tacos. Have you been to Taco Surf yet?"

"It was the first place we went."

We laughed at our tradition of walking across Mission Street and grabbing some of their famous fish tacos. It was usually the first order of business after we arrived.

"I'll see you later by the pool." She handed Teddy to me. "I know you need to check in." She gave me a hug and waved goodbye.

Just as Brooke disappeared, more family members bounded down the hall into the lobby to greet us.

"Hi, Aunt Jillian."

My niece Kaitlin gave me a hug. Two small children followed her and began to hug my legs. Kaitlin is a devoted mother whose children are extremely well-behaved and adorable. Being around them was a treat.

"Where is Silas?"

"He's with mom. She'll probably take care of him the whole time we're here. She's such a great grandma."

"The best. I wish I were one of her grandchildren. How old is he now?"

"He's eight-months and crawling, so he's quite a handful. But Kevin and Sydney help take care of him, so I can't complain."

It can't be easy for her managing three small children while Kenny is in Afghanistan, but she seems to be doing quite well. Of course, it didn't hurt that my brother Daniel insisted they come live with them while he was gone.

Kaitlin is an only child and therefore sole heir to the family fortune, which is growing exponentially online every day.

Daniel had the foresight and perfect timing to start his own business when the idea of building a business online had just started gaining popularity.

They live in a mansion that reminds me of a movie set. In fact, I think that's what it was at one time.

"May we pet Teddy?" asked the children.

"Of course you may." I held Teddy down where they could crowd around and pet him. "Who wants to take him outside to go potty?"

"Children." Kaitlin spoke up. "Take Teddy outside while I talk to Aunt Jillian. After he goes potty, bring him right back. Understand?"

"Yes, ma'am. We understand. Come on, Teddy."

I placed him on the floor and handed Sydney, the oldest, the leash.

"Be careful with him."

I looked at Kaitlin's face and noticed sadness.

"I'm sorry Kenny can't make it this year. He's been to every reunion since you were engaged."

"I know. But he'll be with us next year." She spoke bravely.

I offered a silent prayer that he would return alive and in one piece.

"Well." She shook off her melancholy. "I promised the kids I'd take them swimming, so after they bring Teddy back, we'd better get to it."

The children returned with Teddy, all safe and sound. They handed him over.

"We'll see you later, Aunt Jillian. You, too, Teddy!"

"Bye, Teddy." The kids all gave him one last pat before turning and heading for their rooms to change.

I put Teddy inside his tote and looked toward the front desk. People were still lined up waiting to check in, and I wondered whether or not I should get in line. I had never seen the hotel so busy! The decision was made for me as my mother entered the lobby to greet us.

My mother, Grandmother Lovejoy, was just as vibrant as she had been a year ago. At eighty-seven, she was an icon among her family and friends. She had to be one of the friendliest souls I knew — sincerely interested in every person she met. She even remembered the names of the hotel workers.

"Hi!" she said, excitement in her voice. I loved the way she always smelled of *Red*, her favorite fragrance. I've always worn a fragrance of some kind to emulate her in that way.

She hugged Cecilia and then me. Teddy received a brief nod of acknowledgement. A dog person my mother is not. It's not her fault, really.

When she was a little girl, living on a farm in Wilcox, Arizona, she had a dog. One night, her father put a turkey leg under the house to attract a skunk he was trying to kill. The turkey leg had poison on it, and her dog got to it before the skunk did. That night as she lay in her bed, my mother had to listen to the puppy's death throes. It made such a painful impression on her that she never wanted anything to do with dogs again.

"Have you checked in yet?" She took a look around the lobby. "Where did all these people come from?"

"Guests, like us, I suppose," I said. "Maybe it's another family reunion. I'm in no hurry, but Cecilia doesn't feel well, so I want to get into our rooms as soon as possible." I glanced at Cecilia and noticed she looked a little green.

My mother looked quite concerned. "Would you like to lie down in my suite until Jillian gets you checked in?"

Cecilia appeared relieved. "If you wouldn't mind."

"Jillian, you and Teddy check in. I'll take care of Cecilia. Come, dear. We're right around the corner."

I nodded. "Thank you, Mother."

"Oh, by the way," she said, "the family meeting is tonight at six in the Cayman Room. Bring whatever you want to eat. I'll see you later."

"I think I'll just order some pizzas and have them delivered," I said.

Mother turned and took Cecilia's arm, supporting her. "Come, Cecilia. I'm going to make you a nice cup of tea."

Cecilia followed gratefully.

I turned to face the line at the desk and realized I must wait a few more minutes. I decided to check out the live webcam showing the beach below the hotel. The screen sat over the hospitality table which held the guestbook and information about the hotel, including local events. One flyer stood out to me. It was hot pink and announced a photo shoot tomorrow.

VICTORIA STERLING will be here!!!
Afternoon photo shoot, with signatures afterward.

A headshot displayed an older teen with long, flowing hair. Her face, peering out from beneath bangs, was that of a cross between a girl and a woman. I had never heard of her, but then again, how many stars could I even name these days? Especially young ones like this girl in the photograph.

I refocused my attention on the webcam showing people walking on the beach, children building sandcastles, and surfers in wet suits riding the waves. California beaches aren't the warmest in the world, but the overall climate makes up for the coolness when staying at resorts. A blanket of fog still hovered over the ocean, refusing to let the sunshine through. The atmosphere felt strangely glum, and I had to force myself to shake off the gloom.

This was a happy event, I reminded myself.

But I still felt uneasy.

3 Lobby Drama

The desk clerk, whose nameplate read Angelina, was a lovely young woman with long black hair worn neatly in a ponytail. Her smile radiated warmth and competence.

"I'll be with you in a moment," she said as she checked in a large family. There must have been seven children.

This only reminded me of the fact that I had none.

Teddy wiggled to get down on the floor. He plopped down to wait patiently.

Young families, as well as people from all over the world, came to San Diego as tourists. But this hotel in particular was popular for family reunions.

Angelina answered the phone.

"It's a lovely day here at The Pacific Terrace Hotel. How may I direct your call?"

Quite a few people were checking in. Two gentlemen were next, talking to one another in German. One of them had a surfboard. I'm sure people from all over the world came here to surf. Pacific Beach was definitely a surfer's paradise. There were young and old surfers everywhere you looked. Restaurants, bars and surf shops catered to that clientele, as well as tattoo parlors and second-hand clothing stores.

As we waited, a small party entered the lobby, creating even more congestion. But these guests were different. They must have been celebrities of some kind because the desk clerk excused herself from checking in the family with seven children and came out from behind the desk to greet them personally.

The concierge continued to check in the family. I continued to wait patiently.

Angelina was checking the celebrities in, and I could tell she was thrilled they were staying here. I glanced at the table beneath the webcam and remembered the stack of flyers.

It must be her.

Another young woman, rather plainly dressed, along with a slightly older man and another woman whom I judged to be her parents, accompanied the starlet. A blond gentleman wearing a light gray suit followed the entourage. He must have been either an agent or some other businessman connected with the starlet.

But really, we were all taken with Victoria Sterling, a cross between a pixie and a vixen. A pixie, because of her size, standing only about five feet tall, and a vixen, owing to her lovely face, long strawberry blond hair and the provocative smile she wore. She didn't say a word.

Even the children seemed aware that they were in the presence of a celebrity. They, too, stared at her. The German surfers smiled appreciatively, conscious she must be someone of importance.

I could tell she was used to the attention. She smiled and batted her eyes at everyone as the bellmen loaded an enormous amount of luggage onto the cart and led them to the lobby elevator.

Two hotel workers, wearing tan uniforms and transporting electronic equipment of some kind, moved out of the group's way so the guests could use the elevator first.

Miss Sterling's group entered the elevator, looking past the workers as if they didn't exist. Everyone in the lobby, including me, watched until the elevator doors closed, as if we had just witnessed a moment in history. When the elevator returned, the two men with their equipment got in and descended.

It was finally my turn to check in. Usually our rooms were all together on the ground level around the pool, but this year, other guests had booked one of the rooms, so now Cecilia and I had rooms on the third floor. We did have an ocean view, however, so we couldn't complain.

I stepped up to the desk clerk.

"Welcome back, Mrs. Bradley, and you, too, Teddy."

"Thank you. It's always a pleasure staying here."

"Would you like the wine service this afternoon, Mrs. Bradley?"

"Yes. Thank you. I'll have the red, please."

"Yes, ma'am. And for Mrs. Montoya?"

"I'll have her check later — she's not feeling well at the moment."

"That will be fine," said Angelina. "I'll have it delivered at four o'clock. Enjoy your stay here at The Pacific Terrace Hotel."

Teddy wagged his tail as if to say he was going to enjoy his stay.

I kissed the top of his little brown head, reassuring him he was safe in his new environment.

The bellman pushed our cart to the elevator, waited for me to enter, and closed the door. He took me to the third floor and down the hall to room 316.

I hung up my clothes and put my things away, then admired the room.

It was unlike any hotel room I'd ever stayed in. It was so inviting — I felt like I was in the tropics! The queen mahogany beds were estate size, covered in green and red tropical print spreads. A tapestry hung on the wall between the two beds, and the dark-shuttered doors led to a lovely balcony outfitted with two chairs and a small table.

The bellman left and I walked outside. Teddy squirmed a bit in my arms but soon calmed as we breathed in the fresh and invigorating salt air. Down at the pool, the family with the seven children were splashing and squealing with delight — having a good time.

Perhaps the third floor wouldn't be too bad. What a view!

I made my way downstairs to let Cecilia know her room was ready.

This hotel had always been such a safe environment to stay in, we all propped our doors open with the latch lock so we could flit about from room to room. Mother's door was propped open, so I simply announced a hello as Teddy and I entered.

Cecilia sat in a chair in the corner, which I took as a good sign. But when she looked up at me with circles under her eyes I wondered if she had the flu. Her skin looked rather pale and clammy. Poor thing.

"Hi," she said.

"How are you feeling?" I lay down a towel on the foot of my mother's bed for Teddy.

"A little better, I think. All checked in?"

"Yes. But you missed the lobby drama."

My mother became alert. "Did someone fall?"

I laughed. "No. There's a young starlet by the name of Victoria Sterling who's staying here. She checked in right before we did. I think she brought her whole entourage with her. I read a flyer by the webcam about her that said she's doing a photo shoot tomorrow afternoon down by the pool."

"I'm sure Chase will be interested," said my mother. "You know how he is with pretty girls."

We laughed.

"Have you had lunch, Mother?"

"Please don't mention food," said Cecilia.

Mother and I looked at each other.

"It looks like I'd better get her settled in her room," I said. "I'll call you as soon as I can."

"Good idea. Cecilia, I hope you feel better. Jillian, don't forget to take Teddy with you."

"I won't, Mother." I picked Teddy up, helped Cecilia up from the chair, and let her lean on me. We walked slowly to the elevator.

After I settled Cecilia in her room, suggesting she lie down for a while, I went to my room and called my mother. She wasn't hungry. Since Cecilia was down for the count and couldn't watch Teddy for me, I got him situated so he could take a nap. I ordered room service and checked e-mails while waiting.

Lunch arrived in twenty minutes since most of the restaurants were close by. Even though the Cobb salad was nice, I ate only half. By eating only half of everything, I kept my weight under control and still had the freedom to eat anything I wanted.

This year, since I wasn't staying on the same floor as my family members, I decided not to prop my door open as they would. It felt a little isolating to pull it shut and turn the bolt — as I would in any other hotel situation — but soon enough there was a knock.

Cecilia stood in the hallway, smiling. She no longer looked grayish-green.

"Looks like the nap did you some good. Come on in."

"I'm okay now. I don't think I have the flu or anything. I'll watch Teddy while you go visit with your family."

"Are you sure? I can wait until the meeting tonight if you'd like a little more time."

"No, I'm fine. Really. You go on."

"Okay. Thanks. Order room service for you and Teddy for dinner tonight, and let the front desk know if you'd like the wine service for this afternoon. I'll be having dinner with the family tonight down in the Cayman Room. We always bring food in to share."

"That sounds great. I'll see you sometime tonight, if not before. I'll take Teddy for a walk after his nap. I'm sure the fresh air will do me good."

"Thanks, Cecilia. I'll be off then. See you later."

Only a few minutes to check out the gift shop before going out by the pool to visit. The shop was small but full of wonderful clothes and accessories.

Ironically, the blonde gentleman — the one who was part of the Sterling entourage — stepped out into the hallway at nearly the same moment as I did. His room was a few doors down from mine, but instead of joining me at the elevator, he took the stairs. Probably wanted to get some exercise.

Was their whole group on the third floor? The penthouse and large suites were here. We'd once had a party in one of them. The bathroom had a Jacuzzi tub and the living room a full bar. Perhaps Victoria Sterling was old enough to drink legally, although she didn't look old enough to me.

I rode the elevator to the first floor, walked past the Caribbean Room, and down the hall into the little gift shop adjacent to the lobby. No one was inside, but the desk clerk could see I was shopping. She smiled.

On the first rack, I found a cute skirt and top that would be fun to wear to Casa Guadalajara. I asked to try it on. Right before stepping into the guest bathroom to do so, I bumped into my nephew Chase, my sister Brooke's son.

"Hi, Aunt Jillian," he said. He was in his blue and white bathing suit and nothing else, typical of standard hotel dress.

We hugged. He looked so handsome and grownup. I told him so, and asked how he was doing.

"I'm fine. Mom sent me to come and look for you. I was going to find out which room you were in."

"Is she by the pool?"

"Yeah, everybody's there. Get your suit on and come sit with us. I'll go tell Mom I found you."

"Tell her I'll be there soon. I just had to check out the

gift shop, you know."

"I know." He smiled. "We'll see you later."

What a good-looking young man he is — tall, fair, winsome smile. And Chase is a real charmer. Everyone loves him. Brooke is so proud of the way he enlisted in, and actually made it through, basic training.

I was quite proud of him, too. It did interest me though to think about what he would wind up doing as a career. A lawyer, perhaps? He certainly had the social skills.

The outfit was a perfect fit. I took it to the front desk and asked for it to be put on my tab.

"Of course, Mrs. Bradley," said the concierge. "I'll take care of it right away."

The concierge's name was Natalie Taber. She was fairly young, well-groomed, and wore her red hair long and straight. I judged by her fair skin and green eyes that she had some Irish blood flowing through her veins. Natalie was no more than forty and seemed to take her job very seriously. I hadn't even told her my name, yet she knew me.

I smiled warmly. "I see we have a celebrity staying here."

"Victoria Sterling." Natalie entered my purchase into the computer without looking up. "She's doing a photo shoot tomorrow afternoon at four o'clock by the pool. We have guests staying here just to meet her."

"That must be why it's so busy then," I half said to myself.

"We do this type of promotion on occasion. Their rooms are comped, but it really brings in the business."

"People like staying where the stars are, I suppose."

"Yes, they do. You're all set. I've charged the clothes to your room. Feel free to shop anytime, Mrs. Bradley. And if you need me to unlock the shop anytime, let me know."

"Thank you Natalie, I will."

As I finished up with the purchase, the blond gentleman

I'd seen before with the Sterlings entered the lobby. He smiled tersely and exited through the front door.

I couldn't help my curiosity. "Is that Miss Sterling's agent who just passed by here?"

Natalie looked up for a moment. "Ah, no. That's her personal physician, Dr. Reed Griffin. The other gentleman in the party is her father, Lee Sterling. Is there anything else I can help you with?"

She seemed a bit perturbed for some reason.

"No, thank you." I was a little embarrassed by my question. "Just curious. You don't get to see a star every day."

"I know what you mean."

She picked up the phone to answer a call. It must have been from a guest since there was no ring.

Natalie's smile faded.

"Yes, Mrs. Sterling." Natalie nodded as if Mrs. Sterling could see her. "I'm so sorry and I do apologize. I'll call someone to have that fixed for you right away. Thank you for your patience and I do apologize once again."

Without even glancing up, she dialed maintenance, and within one minute, one of the hotel workers materialized and reported to the front desk. He was one of the men who had been at the elevator taking the electrical equipment down to the garage when I first arrived.

"Zach, Mrs. Sterling can't get her light to work. It's probably just the wrong switch. Take a new bulb with you and take care of it for her. She's in room 312."

The young man nodded and hurried away.

I turned and saw my brother Will come into the lobby. His face was downcast. He was so distracted he almost ran into me.

"Will! When did you arrive?"

"Hi, Jillian. We checked in about an hour ago. Good to see you."

I smiled and gave him a hug.

He seemed to relax a bit. "Lexis lost her room key, so I'm getting her another one. You know how she is."

"A little scatterbrained?" I chuckled. "It's just her age. All girls are like that."

"But she's not a teenager. You'd think someone with a law degree could keep track of a room key."

"I know, but she's having fun with her cousins and isn't thinking about details. Anyway, you're a good dad to get her another one."

"Thanks. Have you been to the pool yet? Everyone is there."

"Not yet. It's my next stop, though. How's Annika these days? I heard she and her fiancé broke it off."

"That was hard on her. He was a real piece of work! I wonder if those girls will ever get married."

"Nowadays, young people take their time."

Will shook his head knowingly and lowered his voice.

"Yeah, they don't want to wind up divorced like their father."

"You never heard anything from Stephanie after she left, did you?"

"Not a word. Hey, let's forget it — it's water under the bridge, as they say. I plan on enjoying myself at this reunion so let's not talk about her, if you don't mind, dear sister."

"Fine. Tell you what. Let's hang out together as much as we can, seeing as we're both single. Deal?"

"I'd like that." He asked Natalie for another room key, and she provided him with one.

He apologized.

"No problem, Mr. Lovejoy."

"Well," he said, "I'd better get to the pool and give Lexis her key. She asked me to hurry. I'll see you later."

"I'll be there soon. Take care, Will."

I felt sorry for Will. He had been divorced ever since his girls were toddlers. His wife wasn't able to handle the work and stress of fraternal twins and walked away one day without a word.

After seven years of hearing nothing from her, Will reluctantly divorced her and felt remorse ever since as if it was his fault somehow that she left.

He did the best he could raising his daughters by himself, but it was difficult, especially since they were girls. Will loved flying, but after his wife left he decided he needed a less dangerous job because of the girls.

He became an online tax expert, started three different companies, all doing the same thing, and generated huge income streams. He was smart, serious and enjoyed the solitude of working on his computer.

Lexis and Annika went to a strict boarding school, and Will believed he had done the best for them. He had no regrets at the way he raised them, even if Lexis did seem a bit more headstrong than her sister.

4 Poolside

Natalie had placed my new outfit in a bag for me, so I gathered it up and headed toward the pool. It didn't seem like the right time to put my bathing suit on — there would be plenty of time later.

The Caribbean Room was buzzing as the staff set up decanters of lemonade and ice water for the guests. I paused to get a glass of lemonade to take to the pool. Guests were sitting at the umbrella-covered tables talking or playing cards. Others laid on the chaises, relaxing in the lovely setting. A few munched on snacks they had brought with them.

Many of my family members sat around the hot tub or laid on the terry-covered chaises. They all waved.

Then began the rounds of greetings, hugs and comments on the way my nieces and nephews had grown since last year.

All the kids were in the pool, playing with beach balls or floating on plastic inflatables.

We loved this place.

Heads turned as Victoria and her friend entered the pool area. There was a new girl with them, one who hadn't been with them when they checked in. Probably a friend or coworker.

They chose the cabana farthest from the other guests in the left hand corner of the pool area.

Victoria wore a red bikini and huge sunglasses. Her skin glistened with sun tan oil.

Her original friend, on the other hand, wore a simple one-piece blue bathing suit the same color as the pool water and a large floppy sun hat. Was she trying to be inconspicuous for some reason? The new friend wore a yellow bikini similar to the one Victoria wore. The friends sat on either side of the starlet. The term ladies-in-waiting came to mind.

I noticed people frequently glanced their way and, like me, found it difficult not to stare.

Victoria seemed content with the attention and the half smiles as she ordered a hotel worker to fetch fresh terry chaise covers.

The worker moved quickly to get the covers and placed them over the chaises.

Our family got our own and put them on ourselves.

The two girls adjusted their chaises to comfortable sitting positions. Victoria placed her sunscreen and binder — a script perhaps — on the small table next to her. She lay face up toward the sun, which barely shone through the cloudy afternoon.

I did hope it wouldn't be overcast the whole time we were here, but even if it was, our family would have a marvelous time just being together.

I looked past the glass walls of the pool area and saw couples strolling hand-in-hand down the boardwalk. They occasionally peered in to look at our pool area. My deceased husband and I had held hands whenever we went anywhere together.

I missed him.

People of all ages rode by on bicycles, and a few dog walkers passed by. All looked content to enjoy their visit to the Pacific Beach area. Overhead, seagulls in formation flew along the ocean shore. Their squawks and squeals floated back toward us on the breezy currents of the air.

Heads turned once again, only this time it was to observe a man I'd noticed in Victoria's group, still dressed in his suit, come onto the patio. He was followed by two people I presumed to be her parents.

All three sat down at an umbrella-covered table where they were in full view of Victoria and her friends. Perhaps they were being protective of their investment.

After the three were seated and a server took their drink orders, gazes returned to Victoria. Even the server couldn't help but glance Victoria's way to see if she needed anything. She summoned him to her with a brief nod.

I walked over to the hot tub where Chase sat with two pretty girls I had never seen before.

"Hi, Aunt Jillian." He smiled ever so charmingly. "Meet Brandy and Katie. Ladies, this is my aunt, Jillian Bradley."

I greeted the girls as Chase stood up. I noticed his mind was not on our conversation as he looked toward Victoria and her friends. I could see he was interested in meeting them, and I knew he was formulating a plan by the way his lips upturned in a smile when he spoke.

"I think I'll take a dip. I'll catch you later Aunt Jillian... ladies."

"Enjoy." I smiled to myself as he sauntered past the starlet and her friends.

He was a cool one, this nephew of mine. He smiled at them but didn't speak or acknowledge that he knew who Victoria was in any way. He dove masterfully into the deep end, just close enough so the water would conveniently splash them a little.

After rising to the surface and noticing he'd gotten them a little wet, he apologized and offered to get dry towels.

The girls seemed amused instead of angry. I could understand how they would be. Chase was an accomplished flirt and knew exactly what he was doing.

If I had been the girls' age, I would have flirted with someone like that. He took after his father.

The doctor and Victoria's parents waited with impatient expressions for their drinks. Though the doctor and mother were head-to-head in conversation, the father glanced at his watch and studied the other guests. He looked at everyone except his wife.

Curious.

The doctor said something. The wife giggled. The father was not amused.

Interesting dynamics there.

Then it was time to go until the family meeting later. Another set of rounds, this time for goodbyes and farewells. As I passed through the pool gate, my room key slipped out of my fingers. I knelt to retrieve it, but suddenly, Victoria's father was there. He reached down, gallantly picked it up, and handed it to me.

"I believe you dropped this."

His voice was deep and articulate. He didn't wear a suit like the doctor, but I got the impression he was a businessman of some sort.

"It was clumsy of me. Thank you." I blushed at the attention.

He wore a wedding ring, but had he noticed that I did not?

His wife and the doctor went right on with their animated conversation as if I didn't exist at all. Unfortunately, they were not paying the slightest bit of attention to the nice man, either.

He smiled. "Take care now."

After thanking him, I returned through the Caribbean Room and felt a little uncomfortable. He was a married man!

Careful Jillian, don't even go there.

Over the years, it's been evident that every time I'm attracted to someone it's turned out badly. Could this be an omen? I hoped not. Coupled with the fact that the weather was on the gloomy side, the encounter seemed to weigh down my previously jubilant attitude.

Taking a final look at the pool area before leaving, I saw Chase and the girls laughing. Two other young men had taken Chase's place in the hot tub, so Brandy and Katie seemed content. Then, as if pulled by a magnet, my gaze went to Victoria's father. He was staring at me.

Lowering my eyes, a little embarrassed, I walked into the hallway to the elevator. At the sound of my key unlocking my room door, Teddy began barking.

He stretched his paws up on my legs. I scooped him up in my arms and hugged him gently, "Missed you, sweet doggie. Did you have a good nap?"

Cecilia greeted me. She sat in a chair reading a magazine.

"Yes, he's had his nap, and I took him out front for a little walk."

"How are you feeling?" I pulled out the outfit from the bag and spread it out on my bed.

"I feel fine. New outfit?" She came over to see what I'd bought. "It's lovely."

"I found it downstairs in the gift shop. Couldn't resist. Have you ordered dinner yet?"

"No, but I will. I'm not all that hungry yet, but Teddy is."

Hearing his name, Teddy yipped.

I stroked his fur. "I know, I know. Cecilia will order your dinner soon."

She smiled. "Have you had a chance to see all your family?"

"Most of them. The rest will be at our family meeting tonight."

There was a knock at my door.

"Wine service, ma'am."

"Come in. Would you like me to have him get your glass of wine, Cecilia?"

"Think I'll pass. It doesn't appeal to me right now. But

I'll join you on the balcony if you want to have yours out there."

"You read my mind. I'll put Teddy in his crate so he won't jump over the railings."

We went out onto the balcony overlooking the ocean. We could see the entire pool area from our vantage point. I peered over the railing and saw Chase still flirting with the girls. The Sterlings and Dr. Griffin sat patiently at the same table and watched them.

I felt a strange sensation in my stomach. From the memory of the dropped key incident? Hopefully I wasn't coming down with the flu.

The sun slowly started to sink in the west. I wondered how the coming sunset would look through the still overcast sky.

When I turned around to look at the pool scene, Victoria's father had left the table. Most of the businessmen in our family continued working on their computers during our reunion, so perhaps he was no different. Was his sole business his daughter's career? It was with some parents I knew.

Cecilia joined me. We sat for a moment together looking out on the ocean.

Surfers looked like seals in their wet suits as they dotted the waves. A few sailboats and merchant ships were farther out. Families with young children built sandcastles on the beach. Not many people swam in the cold water of the Pacific. It was the heated pool for our family. The kids loved it, and it was our favorite place to hang out.

I turned toward Cecilia. "How's your father doing these days? Can't believe it was only a year ago he went missing."

"He's doing quite well. Meeting Daisy Larsen was the best thing that's happened to him since Mom died. They're together all the time."

"I'm so happy for them — they were both lonely. I love

her spunk!"

"Oh, me, too. Dad loves her cooking. It wouldn't surprise me if they get married soon. He's probably just waiting for a respectable time to pass since Mom died, and I understand that."

"I think it would be wonderful."

"Jillian, why haven't you ever remarried? You're attractive and smart...."

"And happen to make a large amount of money, which, believe it or not, can be a detriment. It's a type of subconscious threat to a man's ego if the man doesn't earn as much as the woman. Maybe I'm wrong.

"To answer your question, though, there just hasn't been anyone who compares to my husband. There've been a few nice men, but we've always just wound up friends. Besides, I have Teddy here."

Hearing his name, Teddy flexed his ears flat against his head and looked at me intently.

"He's getting hungry."

"I'll order now. Getting hungry myself. Sit here and enjoy yourself."

Cecilia got up and went into the room to peruse the room service menu. She would be awhile. A few restaurants around the hotel deliver and have their menus available in the rooms. That makes it nice for us, and the hotel doesn't have the hassle of maintaining an in-house restaurant.

The cabernet was rich. I felt it's warmth as I savored it. I glanced toward the pool.

Victoria gathered her towel, ready to leave.

Chase stood close as he spoke to her. A date for later on, perhaps? Why wasn't she smiling?

She and her friends slowly came from the gated pool area and approached the table where the doctor and her mother sat. A few words were exchanged and the girls walked inside the hotel. The doctor and the mother continued to sit and talk, not even looking around to see where the father had gone.

I forced myself not to conjure up any fictional scenarios without having met these people. Still, it was strange for an attractive woman like her to spend more time with the family doctor than with her own husband. A danger signal there, or perhaps it was only my imagination.

Teddy squirmed, wanting out of his crate.

"Okay, sweetie, you ready to be out of that cramped little crate?"

He wagged his tail.

The latch popped open. Teddy bounded out and ran in circles to release his pent up energy.

"Does someone want to play fetch?"

Teddy recognized the word and went over to his pile of dog toys. He chose his favorite — a tiny blue and white cat. It was barely recognizable due to all the chewing and fetching it has been through.

He dropped it at my feet, growling, daring me to snatch it away from him.

My fingers walked slowly toward the cat and created suspense as they moved closer to the treasured item. As they were nearly there, I grabbed it from his reach and threw it across the room.

"Fetch!"

Teddy ran as fast as his little legs would carry him to where the cat landed, grabbed it in his tiny mouth, and pranced back to me. He held the cat proudly in his mouth.

"Good dog!"

Tugging on the cat bated him further. He loved it when I'd act like he had too good a grip on it for me to take it from him.

He relaxed his bite. I grabbed the cat away from him and threw it across the room again. "Fetch!"

Again and again we played. It made a good diversion from thinking about Victoria Sterling.

"What a good dog you are, Teddy! You're so smart! I

love you! Now, play dead!"

He rolled over obediently and pawed the air, as if he was dying, then froze in midair.

"Good dog!"

We repeated the exercise three times for reinforcement, then it was time for treats and kisses.

We continued the training session for several minutes until we were both exhausted. He always gave everything he had to perform well, but he also tired out quickly.

After a drink of water, he begged me with his small brown eyes to pick him up and place him on the towel at the foot of my bed so he could take a nap before dinner. He fell asleep immediately, resting his head on his paws.

By this time, Cecilia had placed her order for chicken Marsala and key lime pie for dessert. Just hearing her made me hungry.

Pizza sounded good to bring to the family conference for my contribution, and my nieces and nephews would love it. Cecilia placed the order for the pizza, and I turned on my computer to check e-mail.

The three newspapers I work for knew my vacation was this week — they all held my e-mails. A lot of good that would do since they would be waiting when I returned. But, it was nice to take a break and not feel like I absolutely needed to answer them right away.

Time to kick off my shoes and turn on the TV to see the hotel activities for the week. Scrolling to Sunday's calendar, the flyer I saw in the lobby popped up in full color to announce the photo shoot of Victoria Sterling for four o'clock that afternoon.

There was a bio of her accomplishments to the present day. It looked like she had been in show business all of her life from the lists of schools, academies, and productions she'd been in.

Also included were a few awards of excellence for her performances. It became clear why she was such a prima donna. Not many girls her age had risen to such stardom.

Cecilia's meal arrived, and she took part of it to prepare Teddy's supper. She had ordered the usual well-rounded meal, which is what I usually fed him.

It was time to freshen up and go down to the Cayman Room for the family meeting. After applying a little lip liner, I started on my hair. The phone rang — the front desk informed me the pizzas had arrived. They needed a signature.

Now to catch the elevator.

5 Family Meeting

The elevator was crowded with guests. We smiled at each other as if we appreciated staying at such a beautiful hotel as The Pacific Terrace. A few exited on the Lobby level, and the rest descended to the garage. Some of the wonderful restaurants in this city required transportation to reach them.

I walked into the lobby and noted a stack of pizza boxes sitting on the counter.

A young man wearing long baggy shorts and a faded Pacific Beach tee shirt stood looking at the webcam. He was probably the delivery person.

Underneath his cap, a mop of auburn hair stuck out everywhere. He reminded me of a hockey player — well-built and a tad brawny, looking as if he could handle any tough situation. He wore a huge pair of red and white tennis shoes without laces. Must be the current style.

After picking up a flyer on the table and studying it, he looked up, noticed I'd arrived and snapped his attention to his pizza. He stuffed the flyer into his jacket.

"Four large pepperoni pizzas, ma'am?"

I smiled. "That's me."

His name tag said Josh. He pointed to the invoice and removed his baseball cap to readjust it. A shock of reddish hair fell on his forehead. He pushed it aside with his free hand and put the cap back on his head.

"Sign here, please."

I added a generous tip and signed the bill.

"Where do you want them?"

"Down in the Cayman room. We'll take the elevator. Just follow me."

He picked up the boxes and followed without a word, looking at the floor, seemingly lost in thought.

I unlocked the door to the Cayman Room with my hotel key and held the door for him.

Family members welcomed the pizza and me.

"Just set them on the table, Josh...is that right?"

"How did you...."

"Your name tag."

"Oh...right. Well, thanks for your business," he said rather perfunctorily as he slowly headed outside. Seeing the large number of people in the room he added, "Just call if you need more."

Food was everywhere: Chinese, Mexican, sushi, and the pizzas. But it was the pizza they were really waiting for. All the kids rushed over to get a slice before it was gone. I grabbed a plate, took a small sample of everything, and got a Coke out of the fridge.

"Come sit with us," called my brother-in-law Greg. He was the CEO of a good-sized credit union in the bay area, and a very good husband and father.

Brooke was holding her new granddaughter, Paxton, trying to keep her safe from the other cousins who ran around the room playing chase.

"I will, thanks."

Everywhere I looked I saw my family, and it felt like heaven. We enjoyed our dinner, cleared away the food and gathered in a circle with Grandmother Lovejoy at the head of the table to begin our family meeting.

She stood. The parents all required their children to pay attention.

"Thank you all for coming to the reunion this year. I

never know if it will be my last one or not, so I am very happy to still be with you."

Members of the family nodded and told her that they were happy she was, too.

She continued. "Let's pray and thank God for allowing us to all be together at least one more time."

We bowed. Grandmother Lovejoy led us in a prayer.

"And now," she said, "we will officially begin our Family Meeting. We'll go around the room and tell one important event or milestone that's happened this year."

My brother Will was the closest to her at the table, so he began. "Well, I had a great year in my business. It was actually up from last year, so for that I'm grateful, especially given the slow economy."

Lexis said, "I finally finished my law degree, and I now work as a paralegal for Williams, Saltzman, and Rollins." Everyone congratulated her. Will was obviously very proud of her.

The parade of accomplishments continued around the room — births, new jobs, promotions, and the trips people had taken. The message was clear. Our family had been extremely blessed.

We talked of our plans for the rest of the week and decided to have dinner at Casa Guadalajara on Sunday night. It wouldn't be a reunion for Grandmother Lovejoy without going there. My father had loved the place. We always thought of him whenever we went.

At sunset, we all scrambled to our rooms to put on sweatshirts and jackets so we could watch the beautiful spectacle outside on the patio in comfort.

Cecilia joined us. I carried Teddy with me.

People on the boardwalk paused, almost reverently, to watch the orange orb sink slowly at the Pacific's rim, shimmering with vibrant colors of purple, red, orange, and yellow. Camera flashes from family members lit the palm trees with the sunset in the background — posted on

Facebook within the hour, of course.

As darkness fell, the palms and flowerbeds lit up. Around the pool area, Tiki torches blazed, and many of us pulled up chairs on the patio area so we could visit. Chase, Lexis, Annika, and Kaitlin headed for the hot tub. Ryan and Christina, Scott and Rachel, Kevin, Samantha and Sydney were there already, sitting on the rim dangling their feet in the steaming water. Soft laughter emanated from the group.

The parents left the sliding patio doors ajar so they could listen for their wee ones who had been put down for the night. Grandmother Lovejoy bid us goodnight and said she would join us in the Caribbean Room for breakfast in the morning.

Brooke and Greg followed her to her suite where they would spend some time visiting.

Teddy was happy to sit in my lap. I gently stroked his soft fur. He lay there contentedly, lulled by our conversation.

Victoria, carrying a drink in her hand, and her modestly-dressed friend entered and swiped their keys, unlocking the pool area. They looked over at the hot tub as Samantha, Kevin and Sydney jumped into the pool, leaving some space for them to sit on the rim. Chase locked on to Victoria. I could see him smile his charming smile. The two girls put their towels down on a nearby pair of vacant chaises and stepped into the steaming hot tub.

I turned to Brooke and raised my eyebrows up and down. She smiled in agreement with me that Chase was indeed the biggest flirt we had ever seen.

I sat with my brothers, Will and Daniel, and Daniel's wife, Paige.

Daniel is the peacemaker in our family. He feels the same way about the reunion as I do. We both love the camaraderie and spend lots of time reminiscing about the crazy things we did as children. Poor Daniel. It's a wonder he turned out as well as he did after the way we used to turn off the lights and scare him when our parents were away. He was the youngest.

I took a sip of coffee Paige had brought me from the Caribbean Room. I loved the woman!

"How's your work going?" I asked him. He used to travel all over the state servicing heavy equipment for Caterpillar until he got tired of the traveling and figured out a way to sell parts online. It was a brilliant move that he fine-tuned to include equipment sales as well.

"Can't complain," he said. "I've hired a great staff to take the orders, so now I just check the stats at the end of the day and make sure the service quality level stays high."

I was impressed, knowing the unlimited possibilities there are on the internet. "So that's why you and Paige get to travel the way you do."

"Yeah, I can run my business from anywhere. The staff are all remote, so there's no overhead whatsoever. How are you doing?"

Daniel has always been shy about talking about himself, which is a good quality in a person. It shows me that they're comfortable with who they are and don't have a need to impress anyone. Of course, Daniel was the baby — so naturally he received more attention than the rest of us.

That made me stop and think about my life. How *was* I doing? The only sounding boards I had were Teddy and Cecilia.

"I'm okay. My columns are still popular, but I barely have time to answer all the e-mails now. I've thought about retiring soon, but I'm just not ready yet. I also don't want to turn my readers over to a staff. We'll see how this year goes, and if I can't handle all the inquiries by then, I'll find some good gardening sites to refer them to. There are so many now."

Paige listened quietly, glancing now and then at the hot tub where her daughter Kaitlin was.

Victoria and her friend were dangling their feet in the water, still flirting with Chase.

Paige has always been the quiet in-law. Quiet, but with quite a wit. I love being around her because I'm inspired by her true servant's heart. Since she's a phenomenal cook, she runs the kitchen for her church and makes herself available to baby-sit her grandchildren whenever she's needed. She takes them to school or picks them up whenever Kaitlin has a conflict. Even when Kenny is home, Paige is there for her.

Everyone loves to visit Daniel and Paige because it's non-stop hospitality whenever we're there. She prepares fabulous meals (homemade chicken pot pie, cheddar biscuits and apple cobbler, for instance) and is always pouring refills of coffee for us as we sit around the large oak table, watching her grandchildren play all over the house. I always gain at least two pounds whenever I visit them.

Daniel must have been reading my mind. "We're setting up a webcam in the Cayman Room so we can hook up with Kenny. Kaitlin's working on the time frame. I think Afghanistan is ten hours later than California."

"That will be wonderful," I said. I wondered if it would make Kenny and Kaitlin even more homesick, but I suppose soldiers are used to seeing their families like that. It reminded me of how much things have changed since the days where soldiers only received letters from loved ones. Now, people even get married on Skype!

Victoria's mother and the doctor walked in and sat down at a table, joining the other guests sitting around the patio area. The doctor pulled the chair out for the mother, and I thought how nice and well-mannered he was. Victoria's father had not joined them.

Why did I even care? Surely, it was normal at my age to feel flattered by anyone of the opposite sex, married or not, who had paid me attention.

Suddenly there was a commotion at the hot tub.

I looked up in time to see Victoria raise her hand and slap Chase across the face!

Chase took the drink away from her and stood up. He seemed flushed with anger or embarrassed by the exchange. He instantly left the group and walked out of the patio, I presumed to his room.

"My goodness!" said Paige. "I wonder what that was all about. I didn't think slapping was something people still did."

"Neither did I," I said, "but I suppose it still is. I wonder what Chase said to deserve it."

Daniel said, "I'm sure we'll find out. Kaitlin will tell us all about it in the morning."

I casually looked over at Victoria's mother and the doctor and heard snippets of their conversation, or rather snippets of her talking to him. It sounded like ordinary conversation two friends would have. Victoria this...diet... the set...work. The doctor looked at her but didn't really say anything — he only nodded or shook his head while she talked.

She smiled as she talked and seemed quite expressive. Was the doctor in love with her? She was quite attractive.

It was almost ten o'clock, and the pool was closing. Parents wrapped towels around their soaking wet children as they got them out of the pool and patted them dry before heading to their rooms. Chase had not returned.

"Looks like it's time to turn in," said Daniel.

Stifling a yawn, I stood to leave. "Me, too."

"Jillian, we'll see you in the morning. What are your plans for breakfast?"

"I'll head for Kona's and get an order of French toast to go. The walk will do me good."

"Okay. We're going to have breakfast here. It's easier for Kaitlin and the kids. We'll see you in the morning."

When Teddy and I returned to our room, Cecilia was

41

talking to her husband Walter on the phone. I nodded and smiled, gesturing for her to continue. They were so in love, and I'm sure it was difficult being apart.

But she understood how much I depended on her for everything, including Teddy's care, and never complained. Besides, I paid her well. She was worth every penny!

The call concluded and Cecilia returned to her own room, bidding us goodnight. I was glad she felt better. I carried Teddy outside on my balcony and looked over the pool one final time.

A maintenance crew was servicing the area, gathering up towels and chaise covers, emptying trash, and hosing down the pavement getting ready for tomorrow's pool guests.

"Come on, sweet doggie, time for bed." I stepped inside the room and placed him on the towel at the foot of my bed, stroking his soft brown fur.

"I love you."

He relaxed, stretched out his paws, closed his eyes, and fell asleep.

With him out, I drew a hot bath, added the hotel's small bottle of shampoo for bubbles, and stepped into the tub to relax for several minutes.

Better climb out before my skin begins to wrinkle.

After drying off, I sprayed my new Coach Legacy perfume all over so the fragrance would pleasantly engulf my senses, making it easier to fall asleep.

Sliding between the crisp clean sheets and soft down comforter, I reflected on the day. The unfortunate incident between Chase and Victoria came to mind.

Wonder how it will turn out.

If someone slapped me in public, I don't know what my reaction would be. I would probably be terribly embarrassed and very mad at whoever slapped me. Chase found himself in a pitiable predicament. Worse than I could imagine. However, he'd always been pretty canny when it came to surmounting problems.

While trying to get comfortable, thoughts of Chase kept coming to mind. His birth was a miracle. He arrived into this world special delivery. Sonograms showed he was developing outside the uterus instead of inside where he belonged. After many prayers from family and friends, Brooke had an emergency C-section and miraculously, Chase was found inside the uterus, growing and developing normally. The doctors were confounded.

Brooke and Greg knew their son would be special. Chase even wore socks that had Special Delivery on them when he came home from the hospital.

This nephew of mine knew how to charm, and creep into your heart. He was polite, good-looking, and for the most part, sincere. Chase and school never saw eye to eye, but after experimenting with junior college and the military, he chose to get serious about both. He served in Iraq and thankfully came home unharmed.

My nephew is a Marine through and through. He is now disciplined and charming, which makes him attractive to girls. As I pictured him as a little boy the vision faded into sleep.

6 Surprise Guest

Sunday morning seemed like a white pants, yellow top sort of day. My favorite turquoise shell necklace made the outfit. Teddy would have to stay in Cecilia's room since Kona's didn't allow dogs. Still, Kona's was the most amazing place on the boardwalk for breakfast.

The long line that had already formed once I got there was merely a testament to the fact.

The restaurant only took cash, but they were nice about it. 'Not enough? Don't worry. Bring the balance next time you come in.' Yes, hometown manners. I loved it!

Customers sat at tables talking about surfing conditions and golf games. People struck up conversations with strangers while standing in line. Very friendly sort of place.

The cheery proprietor cooked up scrambled eggs adding bacon, cheese, jalapeños and some of his famous skillet potatoes with more cheese, jalapeños, and green onions. His wife, who was always smiling every time I came here, bussed tables and refilled supplies of cups, napkins, salt and pepper.

I ordered a cheese omelet for Cecilia with a side order of buttered wheat toast, French toast for me, and got the order to go. The quantities were enough for four people.

On the return walk to the hotel, couples of all ages strolled hand-in-hand. A few bicycle riders zoomed past, some holding onto the leashes of their running dogs.

Several tourists were out for morning walks. Young adults whizzed past on skateboards, along with occasional runners. Truly, this boardwalk was a promenade of humanity, including myself.

I reached the hotel, slid my room key across the gate and entered, carrying the delicious-smelling breakfast covered in foil, while looking around the patio of the Caribbean Room scouting for family members. But the only group out was the family with the seven children, still in their pajamas, sitting at two tables splitting a giant stack of steaming pancakes. Where had they gotten those? I would have to investigate.

The gardeners were busy with trimming and deadheading. One man was hosing off the pool area, and a woman placed fresh chaise covers and towels at the linen station, getting ready for guests. One of the gardeners looked familiar, and he seemed to recognize me, too. I waved to him and walked over to say hello. His badge said Miguel Ramirez, and I was suddenly very thankful for nameplates, otherwise I would never remember enough names. I certainly wouldn't have remembered his, and that could have been awkward.

"Mrs. Bradley," he greeted, offering his hand. "It's so nice to see you here again. How have you been? Did you bring Teddy?"

I took his hand, but hesitated. It would be hard, but finally half-heartedly explained that the dog he knew had passed away. The Yorkie my niece had given me was with Cecilia at the moment.

"How is your wife?" I asked, remembering she stayed home to take care of their son.

"She's fine. Our son works here part time now. I'll introduce you sometime."

"I'd love to meet him."

"Mrs. Bradley, I still read your column every week and use your tips all the time. Look how beautiful everything is."

"Thank you, Miguel. That really makes me feel good. Well, I'd better get this breakfast upstairs before it gets cold. It was very nice to see you again."

"You, too, Mrs. Bradley. Take care."

I walked through the Caribbean Room to get a coffee to go. Families and couples were gathered around enjoying the breakfast buffet. Mom was sitting with Paige and Daniel, chatting with them. The hotel manager, Henrique Gonzales, came through and warmly acknowledged my mother. She basked in the attention from the suave young man with the well-trimmed beard and longish hair. He did have that daring look about him I'd seen in movie stars.

After a bit of chitchat, it was time to take the elevator to my room. As the elevator door opened, Mr. Sterling stepped out. He was alone. I felt sorry for him, even though his wife might be joining him later. We smiled at each other, and he bid me good morning in a tone a little friendlier than just a polite greeting. I blushed, unable to control my reaction to the obvious flirtation on his part.

What kind of woman was this man used to?

Well, I was certainly no cheap date. Still, any flirtation at my age makes me feel attractive, although feelings for my late husband were still there. The doors to the elevator started to close and he just stood there, looking at me. A shiver ran down my spine, but this time it felt like a sign of danger.

Arriving at my room I put the doorstop in so Cecilia could come in without having to knock. I called her room to let her know I had returned.

She carried Teddy in her arms and handed him to me. He snuggled into my shoulder and under my hair, just like a baby. I even gave him a little kiss on top of his head.

"We went for a walk while you were gone," she said.

"Thanks, Cecilia. Would you like to eat outside on the balcony?"

"Sounds good to me. I need some fresh air."

"How are you feeling?"

"Okay. Still a little woozy. But it's not the flu or anything. At least I'm hungry! Think I'll make me some coffee."

"Why don't I feed Teddy his breakfast while you're doing that?"

Teddy yipped when he heard the word breakfast associated with his name.

"You're such a smart dog, Teddy. You know when we're talking about you, don't you?"

I made him a small breakfast of scrambled eggs, bacon and some morsels of wheat toast. I poured him some milk I had ordered with my lunch yesterday into a small cup I brought with me, and carried the dishes into the bathroom.

"Breakfast, Teddy!"

He scurried into the bathroom where he found his dishes and attacked his breakfast, finishing in record time.

"You were hungry, weren't you boy?"

He belched. Apparently, that was his answer.

"Excuse you!"

Cecilia poured coffee and we took our breakfast out on the balcony overlooking the ocean. What a magnificent day it was!

"There's nothing like Kona's," she said as she ate heartily.

"They give you so much food! I can never eat it all."

"I may eat all of mine. Didn't really eat much yesterday."

That reminded me of her sorry complexion the day before. Sort of shamed me for having so much fun.

"At least you're feeling better. That's good. What are your plans for the day?"

"The usual. Writing an article for the paper on connecting large businesses with smaller ones to promote community awareness. It has to be ready by next week, but it still needs work, especially when it comes to the part about mobile applications. Getting enough information in there for people without it being a wash of data should keep me busy all day. Such a balancing act."

"Well, just order in if you like. I'll be down at the pool and will probably go over to Taco Surf for lunch. Want me to bring you some fish tacos?"

"Thanks, but that doesn't appeal right now. Sorry."

"No problem. Well, off to the pool to see what's going on. Got to find out what happened with Chase after last night."

Cecilia was alert. "What happened?"

I stopped after grabbing my purse. Of course, she didn't know.

"Victoria Sterling. You know, the young starlet. She slapped Chase when they were in the hot tub."

"Wow! Why did she slap him?"

"That's what I intend to find out. He was really embarrassed and got up and left after it happened. It looked to me like she had been drinking."

Cecilia's eyebrows shot up, and I could tell she was running scenarios around in her mind.

I turned. "I'd better get ready for relaxing. I do love it here!"

My black one-piece bathing suit was still waiting for me in the bag. Swimming was not my passion, and this particular suit had lasted me for ten years since I never got it wet. After pouring myself into its stretchy fabric and admiring the illusion of a thinner me, I covered the whole thing up by pulling a black lace cover up over my head. Sunscreen came next in the arsenal to protect my fair skin. Then I ran a comb through my hair, subconsciously wanting to look my best for...no, I would resist thinking about Lee. He was a married man for one thing, and it's wrong even to have thoughts about such a person.

To help, I muttered a quick prayer, "Forgive me, Lord."

Thankfully, my head instantly cleared and I spritzed myself with perfume. My thoughts returned to Cecilia who was still in my room, waiting patiently.

"I'll check with you after lunch to see how you and Teddy are doing," I said. "Call me if you need anything. Oh, and by the way, there's a photo shoot for Victoria Sterling at four o'clock down by the pool. I'd love it if you'd bring Teddy down then."

Cecilia smiled knowingly. "Sure. You go and have a good time with your family. And don't worry about Teddy. We'll go for another walk after a while."

"Thanks, dear. You're an angel — I'll see you later. Goodbye, precious dog." I nuzzled, giving him two kisses trying to make up for being gone all morning.

My wide-brimmed straw hat, trimmed with a zebra print scarf, gave me an air of sophistication in addition to protecting me from the sun's damaging rays. It matched my zebra-tote full of sunscreen, sunglasses, room key, and a book. As I reached the door to the main patio, I put on my sunglasses and headed confidently for the pool.

The crowd in the Caribbean Room had thinned a bit since the breakfast service had ended. The sun had not burned off the fog entirely, so wearing my sunglasses was a bit premature. Back into the tote they went. As I passed the threshold, the sun began to bathe me in warmth and the cool ocean air caressed my face. I remembered my husband. He used to caress my face in a similar way with his warm hand, telling me how much he loved me.

The gardeners were finished tidying up the landscaping and had disappeared. There were a few empty cabanas and, hopefully, one of them had my name on it. I ran my key card through the pool gate and entered. The gate creaked a little reminding me of my right knee sometimes.

The linen kiosk was full of fresh white towels and chaise covers, so I took one of each, found an empty cabana, set my tote beside the chaise, spread the cover over it, and sat down to relax. No one else in my family had arrived yet. I removed my wide-brimmed hat and took out my book to read until someone came.

Before finishing the first page, sure enough, Brooke and Greg arrived and hailed me. So much for getting any reading in, but that was usually what happened. There were just too many of my family to visit with. Greg pulled up an extra chair as Brooke went to get a chaise cover and towel.

Greg is fair and wears glasses, but he's also fit and intelligent. Brooke was attracted to him immediately after meeting him in the singles group at their church. He was witty and confident, and even though Brooke had a boyfriend at the time, Greg was a much better catch. Brooke let her boyfriend down gently, and then let it be known to the group that she was available. Greg never had a chance. My sister is a woman who knows how to get what she wants.

"How are you this morning?" I'd been hoping he would mention Chase before I did. He looked tired.

"I'm okay, I guess." His voice sounded deeper than usual. "We didn't get much sleep last night."

Brooke spread the cover over her chaise and plopped down next to me. "It was not fun. Chase was hard to calm down after the incident. He vented to us for at least an hour."

My heart went out to all three of them. "What exactly happened? Did he tell you?"

Greg sighed and looked at me straight in the eyes. "He was trying to help her, and look what happened."

Brooke chimed in. "Jillian, that girl was drunk. Chase said she had started cursing, and there were children around. He said he was afraid she would regret her behavior if she kept going the way she was, so he tried to take the drink away from her. When he tried, she slapped him."

"Slapped him hard, too!" Greg added. "She sounded like

maybe she wasn't drunk after all if she could pack a punch like that. He had a handprint on his face that took several minutes to go away. Wouldn't think a person who was drunk could hit that hard."

"So you think it was an act?"

"Well, she is an actor, after all," said Brooke. "I just hope Chase stays away from her. If he's smart, he will. She's nothing but trouble."

"She sounds spoiled to me," said Greg. "Anyway, I need to get going."

"Greg is playing golf with Daniel over at Torrey Pines in just a few minutes. See you later, dear," said Brooke, as he left. "What are your plans for today, Jillian?"

"Just to stay here and simply relax! Haven't had a chance in quite a while. Taco Surf is definitely on the agenda for lunch one day, but since we're going to Casa Guadalajara for dinner tonight, it can wait. What about you?"

"Watching the kids while Rachel and Christina go shopping. Paxton will go with Christina since she's still nursing. Kaitlin is going with them, too, and she'll take Silas. The kids will want to be in the pool. Shouldn't be hard to watch them."

What an awesome thing it was. My sister volunteering to watch her four grandchildren, ages five through eight, all at the same time. Would I have been able to do such a thing if I'd had grandchildren? It's one thing to look out for my nieces and nephews at my house with their parents on the premises, but to watch four children all at the same time and have all that responsibility? God certainly knew what he was doing when he created parents. It would have been nice, but being an aunt was wonderful. I was fine with the way things were.

The pool began to fill with children, some wearing life jackets, others armed with flotation devices in all shapes and sizes. Dutiful parents swam alongside them, making sure they were safe and secure. The sun finally burned off the fog. Time for sunglasses to shield me from the glare. I had just put them on and reapplied a little sun screen when Will and Annika came through the gate. They saw us, but chose to find a sunnier spot for themselves. Will was wearing a straw Panama hat since he's fair-skinned like me and because he needs to protect his balding scalp. Annika wore a brown print one-piece and cute cover up. She looks nothing like Will and takes after her mother who, as I remember, had beautiful auburn hair. I decided to go to them.

"Good morning," I greeted them cheerfully, "such a beautiful day, isn't it? Where's Lexis? Is she up yet?"

"Hey, Jillian, Lexis is sleeping in. She was out late last night with her cousins, but she'll be down later." Will nodded a hello to Brooke and Greg across the pool. "Chase hasn't come down yet. I heard what happened."

"I'm sure he'll bounce back," I said. "After all, he is a Marine."

Annika spoke up. "Yeah, but that slap could be brutal to a guy's ego. Chase will get over it. You watch. He'll laugh it off, I'm sure."

Then she turned to me. "Are you going shopping with us, Aunt Jillian? A bunch of us are planning to go."

"Not this time. I think I'll just relax by the pool today and maybe take Teddy for a walk later. He'd enjoy getting out a bit more. Besides, Cecilia could use a break as well."

"She wasn't feeling well I heard. How is she?" Annika asked as she slathered sunscreen on her olive skin. Her kind question reminded of the differences between Lexis and Annika.

Annika is attractive in a wholesome all-American girl sort of way. She's an MRI technician at a local hospital and loves her work. She's popular among her peers, has dated young doctors and other professionals like herself. She is in no hurry to settle down, though.

Annika had been engaged once and it ended badly —badly enough for her to still feel regret at being so gullible. Her fiancé had taken advantage of her financially. After Will had him checked out, Annika discovered he was a professional swindler.

She enjoyed going to a party now and again but preferred to stay at home reading a good book instead of leading a wilder life like her sister.

Lexis reminded me of an unbroken horse with her chestnut mane of hair and large defiant brown eyes. She was a beautiful young woman, independent and stubborn.

She had a law degree, worked for the offices of Williams, Saltzman, and Rollins as a paralegal and was happy working there. The job was taxing, but the company treated her well. She also enjoyed the particular work of helping people with medical fraud issues. Making a nice salary didn't hurt either. Following her father's advice, she shrewdly invested part of her earnings before buying clothes and spending money on entertainment. Will was very proud of his girls, especially Lexis, and tolerated the fact that she was still young, unattached, and liked to party.

I heard a ring tone and realized it came from Will's swimsuit pocket.

"Excuse me a minute, Jillian," he said and answered the call.

His face turned from a pleasant expression of ambivalence to concern. Will steadied himself, placed his other arm on the chaise and then he looked at Annika, as if the call concerned her.

"That will be fine," he said. "Three o'clock in the lobby." He ended the call and stared at the ground for a moment. He looked like he was in shock.

"Will," I placed my hand on his arm. "Is everything okay?"

He slowly turned his head toward me and opened his mouth, but nothing came out.

"Dad?" Annika asked. "What's happened?"

He looked at her again and slowly shook his head. "It's unbelievable. After all these years!"

"Will, tell us who that was." I implored.

Will looked away for a moment, trying to gain his composure, and then turned toward us. "That was Stephanie, my ex-wife. After all these years! She's coming here at three o'clock to meet with us."

Annika sat very still, in shock no doubt. "Dad, what does she want?"

Annika's question came out in a whisper.

Will sighed and looked at me. "She says she just wants to see how her girls turned out. She told me she didn't want anything but just to see them."

"And you're going to meet her?"

Somehow, I knew Will had never gotten over her, but I sensed danger.

"Yeah. We're all adults now, right? I'd like her to see that we did just fine without her help."

There was a definite touch of resentment in his voice.

Annika fought the tears which puddled at the rim of her eyes.

Was this the best thing for my nieces? Of course, I didn't have a say. Perhaps it was better to change the subject, give them some time to talk in private.

"Will, I'll be thinking about you. I'll catch you all later. Are you coming to the photo shoot?"

"That depends on how long this meeting will last. If you'll excuse us, we'll go to our room."

We exchanged hugs, then he and Annika left.

At my cabana, Brooke was looking at me intently. I couldn't fool her. She knew something was up with Will.

"Stephanie just called Will." I dropped the news like a bomb.

Brooke looked shocked.

"He's meeting her with Lexis and Annika at three this

afternoon in the lobby."

"Jillian, that's bizarre! It's been over twenty years since she left. What does she want? Did she say?"

I shrugged. "She says she wants to see how the girls turned out. That's all. We'll just have to wait and see what happens. It is pretty bizarre, her turning up like this. Enough! I'm hungry for lunch. Why don't we walk down to The Green Flash? Their Shrimp Louies are fabulous!"

"Sounds good to me, sister dear. I'll change and meet you in the lobby. Let's check with Mom and see if she wants to join us."

"Good idea. See you in a few minutes." We walked out the pool gate and returned to our rooms.

I found Cecilia napping with Teddy who lay on his towel at the foot of the bed. "Sorry to wake you," I said softly.

"Just dozing." She stifled a yawn. "Must be the sea air. At least I'm not feeling woozy anymore."

"Glad to hear that. Would you like to join us for lunch at The Green Flash? They have a nice patio overlooking the ocean, and we could bring Teddy in his tote. It might be good for you to get out of the room for a while."

Cecilia thought for a moment and agreed. "Sounds good. Okay, thanks, Jillian. Who else is coming?"

"Oh, Brooke and maybe my mom. Just need to change my clothes."

"I think I'll go like I am. It's casual, right?"

"Very."

Dressed in my new outfit from the gift shop, I combed my hair and grabbed my purse. "Teddy, let's put you in your tote and go have lunch. What do you say?"

He yipped twice and wagged his tail.

"Promise to behave yourself and I'll give you part of my lunch!"

Teddy flexed his ears at the mention of lunch. Willing to do anything for food, he hunkered down in his tote and the three of us headed for the lobby. What a smart dog he was!

7 Photo Shoot

While I waited in the lobby for Mom and Cecilia, a young man about Chase's age came in and went to the front desk. He was well-dressed compared to most young men his age, and he nonchalantly asked about the photo shoot for Victoria. The concierge directed him to the table holding the flyers and told him how to get to the pool. He thanked her and walked out the front door, perusing the flyer he had in his hands. He almost ran into me, but I quickly avoided the collision.

"Excuse me," he said politely.

"No problem." I smiled.

Seeing Teddy in the tote he said, "Nice dog. It's a Yorkie, isn't it?"

"Yes. His name's Teddy and he's my companion."

The young man nodded and walked out the door to the street. He got into a dark gray Civic and promptly drove out of the parking lot.

Fan of Victoria's?

Cecilia and Mom arrived, and we walked a few blocks down the boardwalk, passing the Tower 23 Hotel, which had a high-end restaurant on the ground floor.

We soon reached The Green Flash.

The Maître d' seated us on the cozy open-air patio and we all ordered Shrimp Louies. Perfect fare to eat right next to the ocean. It felt so relaxing to enjoy a leisurely lunch with people I loved, listening to the rhythm of waves rolling in and out, punctuated with the cries of seagulls.

Teddy waited patiently until we were served. I gave him a few morsels to keep him occupied.

"You're such a good dog, Teddy," I told him, "Now lie down in your tote and take a nap while we eat our lunch."

He seemed to understand the command and lay down, then closed his eyes.

Mom wanted to hear about the slapping incident.

I explained the ordeal in a few short sentences.

"I sure hope this doesn't spoil the reunion for him." She sounded worried.

"Chase is a Marine, Mom, I'm sure he'll be fine. He'll be embarrassed for a while, but it will pass."

"I suppose, but I've watched that girl, Veronica...."

"You mean, Victoria?" Cecilia said helpfully.

"Whatever her name is, she's a troublemaker. I watched her at the pool and saw her with several other young men besides Chase."

"When was this?" I asked, surprised at Mom's interest in the starlet.

"You weren't there. And I don't even think those boys were hotel guests. In fact, I watched them come in through the gate. The girl she's with all the time let them in with her key."

Cecilia and I looked at each other in amazement.

"Mom, you'd make a good detective." I chuckled.

"You can laugh if you want, but there's going to be trouble. I can sense it. I've been around long enough to know what I see, and that young woman enjoys men fighting over her. It will come to no good. You wait and see."

"That's very prophetic of you. I hope Chase steers clear of her if you think she's that much of a problem."

We walked back to the hotel, this time with Teddy on his leash to get some exercise. The boardwalk was crowded with tourists and bicycle riders with a sprinkling of various dogs, both on leashes and free. A few dogs were playing Frisbee with their owners on the greenbelts. Teddy wanted to play with every dog he came in contact with, but I kept him on a short leash as we walked.

We came through the boardwalk gate to see who was at the pool. Victoria and her crowd inhabited one of the cabanas. I noticed there were two young men, besides her friend, doting on the starlet, laughing at whatever she said.

The sun was now out and warmed the air to a perfect seventy-five degrees. With the pool heated, it was sheer heaven to be inside or outside of the water. Brooke sat between the pool and hot tub, keeping an eye on Samantha, Kevin, Sydney and Mallory. All four wore flotation devices or played with foam tubes and beach balls. Brooke waved to us as we passed by.

Mom said, "I'm ready for a nap! I'll go and lie down for a while. See you girls later."

After she left us, we walked leisurely to the elevator feeling very much like doing the same.

It was almost four o'clock when I awoke.

Teddy stretched his little paws out in front of him and then shook all over.

Wish I could do the same to get my blood flowing again. I stretched, but I didn't shake.

"Come on, Teddy. You can go with me to the photo shoot if you stay in your tote. Do you want to come?"

He pricked up his long ears and wagged his tail as if to say, 'You bet I do. Let's go!'

The photo shoot was set up on the patio outside the doors of the Caribbean Room. On a large table holding a giant poster of Victoria, a pile of black and white glossy photos were ready to be autographed.

A photographer holding a complicated-looking camera with a telephoto lens was positioned perfectly to capture adoring fans getting autographs. Upbeat music played over the speakers which completed the set, for that was just what the whole scene reminded me of — a set. A line had already formed, and I felt the urgency to line up as well.

Lee Sterling and his wife were seated at a nearby table in full view of the shoot. Victoria's friend sat at another table with a young man from the lobby. I'd seen him earlier. He must have been a good friend to be fraternizing like that.

Teddy was asleep in his tote, obviously bored since there were no other dogs around.

When it came to my turn, Victoria didn't even look up. She asked, "To?" And I replied, "Jillian will be fine." She scribbled:

To Jillian, Always, Victoria Sterling

Underneath, she had signed her character's name:

"Ashlie" — from "It's My Life"

I thanked her even though she still didn't look at me, and the next person in line stepped up.

I found an empty table and put Teddy in his tote down on the chair next to me. He slept on as I scoured the group unobserved behind my dark glasses.

Lee's wife was watching Victoria sign photos, and Lee was watching...me! I didn't flinch but it made me a little uncomfortable, to say the least.

Victoria's doctor didn't appear to be around anywhere, which struck me as unusual. Perhaps he had other patients besides her.

Lee stood and kissed his wife on the cheek. I heard her say, "Have a good trip, dear."

Was he leaving the hotel?

"See you tomorrow," he said.

Lee walked to Victoria's table and told her goodbye, blowing her a kiss from his hand. She did look up for a brief moment and smiled, but when the next fan approached, she lowered her head again.

Chase waited in line to get a photo as well. It surprised

me. Got to admire his spunk to get past the insulting slap episode. But, what would Victoria's reaction be?

She looked up when it was Chase's turn. I could read her lips when she saw him.

"Hi, Chase," she said, smiling almost sheepishly it appeared to me. As she started to sign the photo and hand it to him, she said something. Couldn't quite make it out, though. The photographer told her to look up and smile at the fan, saying that this was the shot he was looking for. She posed and several shots were taken of the two.

Had she been apologizing?

Chase nodded and stepped away as the next person in line took their turn. Victoria put her head down again, acting as if the fan didn't even exist. But she knew Chase existed. Of that, I was sure.

Several times, Victoria looked over at her friend and the young man from the lobby, but she seemed bored. After an hour passed, and no one else was in line, Victoria stood up and walked over to her friends as the photographer packed up his equipment.

A server approached their table and took drink orders. Something to drink sounded refreshing to me as well, so after the server delivered their drinks, I ordered a Pepsi over ice and a cup of water for Teddy.

The server's name tag said Zach Ramirez. Was this the son Miguel said was working here now? Ramirez was a common last name, so I hesitated to ask him. He was about Chase's age but seemed a bit shy when he took my order. There was only a brief smile in response to mine.

Zach returned with my Pepsi and Teddy's cup of water, and I signed the bill.

Victoria's mother hadn't moved from her table since her husband left even though Victoria had seemingly disappeared with her two friends.

The doctor walked out from the Caribbean Room and straight to Mrs. Sterling. He sat down and the two started

an animated conversation, as if they were best friends.
I still found it curious.

Offering Teddy some water from the cup, which he lapped gratefully, I took a sip of my Pepsi, looked over at the servers standing around, watching for orders to be taken, and noticed Zach looking distracted. His gaze rested on the towel stand. Why wasn't it focused on Victoria like everyone else's? Maybe not every young man was like Chase. That was probably a good thing.

Zach picked up a tray and entered the pool area, offering to take orders from guests sitting around on their covered chaises soaking up the sun. Brooke ordered smoothies for all the grandchildren, and after making their flavor selections, they jumped into the pool where they stayed for a few more hours. How Brooke loved and adored her grandchildren. I could tell they loved and adored her, too.

The doctor and Mrs. Sterling were now having quite a conversation. He seemed to be doing most of the talking.

Teddy got restless and started to pant.

Time to take a little walk.

After catching Brooke's attention and pointing to Teddy, indicating I was leaving, she waved, and Teddy and I walked through the patio, past the doctor and Mrs. Sterling, and out the gate to the boardwalk.

There were a few homeless people here and there, some sleeping on benches, others rummaging through trashcans looking for cans to recycle for cash.

I felt alone but was grateful that at least Teddy was with me, and he *did* make me smile.

A guitarist was strumming softly up ahead where a few onlookers had gathered. We stopped for a moment on a grassy stretch so Teddy could relieve himself. I noticed a young man sitting not far away holding a medium-size apricot poodle wearing a pink collar.

The poodle was not groomed to look like your

stereotypical show dog, but was clipped short with a puffy crop of hair on top of her head, ears left long and silky, and a pom-pom tail to finish off the look. The dog looked clean and well-cared for. Teddy yipped a hello to the poodle, and the poodle returned a bark.

The owner of the dog looked up from where he sat and smiled briefly at us. I felt the camaraderie at once. The man looked to be in his mid-thirties, but it was hard to tell how old he really was.

Compared to most of the scantily-clad beach lovers dominating the boardwalk, he was neatly dressed in a tropical print shirt and khaki slacks. His hair was streaked from the sun, as if he spent a lot of time outdoors.

Must be a surfer.

"Nice dog," he said. "What's his name?"

"Teddy," I told him. "What's your poodle's name?"

"You mean you can tell she's a poodle?" He chuckled. "That's pretty good since she isn't clipped like one. Her name is Fancy."

"Well, it's nice to meet you, Fancy." I reached down and let Fancy smell my hand. When she was comfortable with me, I petted her fur and then gently scratched behind her ears.

"Shake hands, Fancy," her owner commanded gently. Looking timidly at him, Fancy stuck out a shaking front paw. I took it gently and shook it twice, then asked Teddy to reciprocate. After two tries, he succeeded in shaking the man's hand. We both smiled lovingly at our pets.

Since I was not sure of the owner, there were no introductions. Besides, he seemed caught up listening to the lilting song the guitarist played. He also didn't seem interested in introducing himself, so we just left it at that.

The guitarist continued filling the air with pleasant music as Teddy finished his business. The leavings went straight in the doggie bag I always carried with me on walks.

To pass the time I made conversation again. "How old is Fancy?"

"I'm not really sure. I think she's pretty young, though. She sort of adopted me about two years ago. She's a smart dog. She'll dance for a piece of chicken. She's a little skittish until she gets to know you, and she's afraid of cats. It's been interesting."

He sounded intelligent, and I found myself becoming interested in who he was.

"Sounds like it," I replied. "Teddy doesn't like cats, but he'll tolerate them if he has to. I'm curious. Have you ever been to the Surf Dog Competition up at Del Mar? I saw the billboard about it when we came in yesterday."

"Yeah, but just to watch. Fancy doesn't like the water and I don't either."

"I see. So what do you like to do around here?"

I asked this before thinking it was really none of my business! He didn't seem to take offense.

"We just hang. It's a good place to hook up, if you know what I mean."

"I understand."

He must mean meeting girls.

"Well, I'd better be getting along. It's almost time to get ready for dinner. Fancy, it was nice to meet you."

"And Teddy, it was nice to meet you, too," he said. "We'll see you around."

Teddy yipped again and Fancy stared at us until we entered through the boardwalk gate.

How did that young man support himself? Was he a college student? Was he as lonely as me?

We arrived home at The Pacific Terrace just as Christina, Rachel and Kaitlin returned from shopping, loaded down with packages.

"You bought out the stores!" I joked.

"Yeah, we had a great time," said Kaitlin.

"Here, Kaitlin. Let me hold Silas while you take those

packages to your room."

"Thanks. He's heavy — you'd better sit down to hold him. Your back isn't strong."

I sat down as ordered. Kaitlin handed me the baby and I held him gently to my chest.

He smelled so sweet. How soft he was!

Teddy woofed, a tiny bit jealous.

Kaitlin's room was just a few steps away and it only took a moment before she returned. She momentarily looked relieved, and the reason was apparent immediately. This child *was* heavy!

"We had such a great time. I love the shopping here," she said. "Are we going to Casa Guadalajara tonight?"

I began to bounce Silas on my knee, and it made him chuckle.

"That's the plan. Let's meet in the lobby at six-thirty so we can work out the transportation. Spread the word."

"Okay. Have to put these kids down for a rest if we don't want fussy babies in the restaurant."

Kaitlin reached for Silas, and I reluctantly handed him to her. Teddy jumped up and down for me to pick him up and I did, reassuring him that the baby wouldn't be taking his place.

"See you later, Aunt Jillian. Thanks for holding him for me."

"It was a pleasure. He's a wonderful baby. Come on, Teddy, let's go see what Cecilia's up to."

Casa Guadalajara has been a favorite restaurant on our family's agenda since our father first started bringing us here ten years ago. We've dined in their beautiful courtyard with its splashing fountains, in their gorgeous dining room, and in the romantic setting of the garden room. The variety of settings and the extensive menu keep us returning.

I glanced at the menu. "Dad was so proud of his family and loved having us around him, especially in public like this where he could show us off."

"I remember. What are you having, mom?"

"I think I'll have my usual."

Mom always ordered the enchiladas verdes de pollo (chicken enchiladas with green sauce), but I ordered something different every time, since the menu offered such unique choices.

I chose the Puerto Nuevo Trio, a magnificent combination of Puerto Nuevo-style lobster, bacon-wrapped shrimp and fresh sea bass grilled in butter, garlic and cilantro, served with arroz poblano and ensalada of julienne vegetables with lime-cilantro dressing. And a glass of Sangria, since this was a special occasion.

After ordering, Brook handed her menu to the server.

"Do you remember last year we saw Loni Anderson glide into the restaurant?"

Loni Anderson was a popular TV star in my day.

"Yes, I do. I still remember her escort followed at a respectable distance. There was quite a buzz when she entered. It was a moment I'll never forget. She had a huge number of friends to celebrate her birthday."

The mariachi band was performing this evening, which lent a special atmosphere to the colorful restaurant in Old Town. All of us sat at one long table so we could be together.

Good times. Mom lives for this moment each year, having her family all around her. She has told me it's her purpose in life now, to keep our family together.

The thought of Will's wife Stephanie, and how hard Mom tried to help her with the twins, came to mind. Unfortunately, Stephanie was too proud to accept her help.

As a result, Stephanie had failed miserably as a mother. Her own mother was not a part of her life by choice. Unfortunately, her mother was an alcoholic, living in an institution the last we heard.

And now, Stephanie wanted to see her girls again. Understandable. What had happened when they met this afternoon? I looked down the table at Will and was surprised that he was actually smiling for a change. Lexis and Annika were not.

Brooke, sitting next to me, nudged me with her elbow to look at the party coming into the restaurant. In walked Victoria Sterling and her entourage: Her mom, doctor, friend and boyfriend, we all assumed. He was the same young man who sat with her friend during the photo shoot this afternoon.

Victoria was dressed in filmy white — an off-shoulder ensemble accessorized with large gold earrings and spike heels. Her makeup looked theatrical, and everyone in the restaurant looked at her. As she passed our table, she waved briefly to Chase. He blushed royally. The hot tub incident seemed to be in the past now.

The party walked to the patio and the host seated them at a center table, for the entire world to admire, no doubt.

Brooke turned to Chase and gave him a questioning look. "So, you're back in Victoria's good graces."

Chase blushed again.

"Everything's fine. She apologized for slapping me. I'm going to a party up in her suite tonight — she invited me and told me to bring anyone I wanted." He looked up and down the table and asked, "Anyone want to go with me to a party tonight?"

Lexis raised her hand. "Me! Annika, come go with us, please?" Annika hesitated but finally agreed.

"I guess I'll go and keep an eye on you two," she said reluctantly.

The servers came and set our wonderful meals down

before us, while the mariachi band serenaded Victoria and her party. When they had finished, the band came to our table.

Hearing them sing beautiful songs with such feeling, such passion, was a real treat! We ate sopapillas with honey for dessert, ordered coffee, and enjoyed watching the children just being children.

After dinner, we strolled through Old Town, looking into shops that sold all kinds of handmade Mexican crafts.

There was a lovely turquoise-studded silver necklace that I had been looking for. The necklace would go with a pair of silver earrings that Prentice, a friend from Clover Hills, gave me for my birthday last year.

Prentice owns an art gallery where I love to shop. He and I have dinner together on occasion and enjoy each other's company — nothing serious. On my part, anyway.

The shopkeeper wrapped the necklace carefully, placed it in a bag, and handed it to me.

None of the art galleries in Old Town interested me. I preferred art that was more contemporary, and my walls at home were covered with beautiful paintings.

The others were ready to return to the hotel and put the young ones down to sleep so we could watch the sunset. Afterward, we would gather on the patio and enjoy each other's company under the twinkling palm trees.

Except for the incident with Chase in the hot tub, the reunion had been fun.

So far.

8 Double Homicide

It was early Monday morning, and the Caribbean Room buzzed with our family filling their plates with delicious pastries, bagels, and fresh fruit. I got some coffee and a plate for myself and found a seat at the table where Mom and Brooke sat, chatting and watching the antics of the grandchildren.

Silas and Paxton were sitting in their high chairs enjoying Fruit Loops, picking them up one by one, and inserting them into their mouths. Kaitlin was getting food for Kevin and Sydney. Rachel and Scott were almost finished eating and started to come over with Samantha and Mallory to say good morning.

Loud voices in the hallway, some shouting orders, others firing questions in Spanish, caused the kitchen staff to disappear into the hallway. All the guests, including Brooke and myself, got up from our tables to see what the commotion was all about.

We watched as police officers pushed two gurneys, ominously holding black body bags, down the hall. As the gurneys clacked noisily on the tile, all I could gather from the snippets of conversation from the staff were the names Victoria Sterling and her mother.

It was shocking! Such a departure from the idyllic calm of enjoying a leisurely breakfast with my family!

Curious mothers took their children inside the Caribbean

Room making way for the gurneys to proceed down the hall, while a few fathers continued to view the spectacle and waited to gather more facts.

There were butterflies in my stomach.

The hotel manager was now on the scene, talking to the officer in charge. They both looked my way. I turned and saw Brooke, her eyes wide with fear, her face pale, and that's when we both realized that Chase could be in trouble.

I went to her and put my arm around her shoulder.

"Don't worry, it's going to be okay."

The manager and officer approached us, and after introductions, the detective, who introduced himself as Mac McKenzie, asked Brooke where Chase was. The man didn't look friendly at all, rather the opposite — stern and spoke a little too forcefully for my taste.

He made me wonder if things really were going to be okay.

Brooke was shaking. "Chase?"

She spoke his name in a whisper. "He's probably still asleep in our room. Why do you ask?"

"Ma'am, we need to talk with him," Detective McKenzie told her gently, but his face was stern. "If you'll take us to him, we would appreciate your cooperation."

The fear and apprehension of what might be coming gripped me, even though the detective simply said he only needed to talk to Chase. Someone must have told the police about the hot tub incident. But who? Victoria's friends, maybe?

Brooke stood more erect.

"I'll come with you, Detective," she said bravely.

I took her arm and said, "I'm coming with you."

Detective McKenzie stopped and looked me squarely in the eye. There was a stern determination in his face to arrest Chase.

"If you'll please wait here, ma'am, I would appreciate it."

"But she's my sister."

"Wait here, please," he said, only this time it was a command.

Brooke looked at me and tried to smile but didn't succeed. I saw the fear in her face. The two of them walked down the hall to her room.

I followed at a distance so the officer didn't notice, hoping to see what happened. It only took a few minutes before they came out of the room. The officer led Chase out the front door of the hotel. Chase was barely dressed in a tee shirt and jeans — his hair wasn't even combed. Brooke and Greg followed, holding on to each other for support as their son was taken away.

Together, we watched, stunned, as the police car drove away with Chase looking at us from the rear window. The look on his face was one of confusion and fear. Chase was really scared.

"Lord," I prayed, "please protect my nephew and bring him home to us. Amen."

After my prayer, Lee Sterling came through the front door wearing a suit and tie as if he was coming straight from a business meeting. He saw me standing with my sister and brother-in-law. He looked shaken with the news that both his wife and daughter were dead. Who wouldn't have been?

Unless that person was the deranged killer.

Greg took Brooke to their room, and I remained in the lobby, unable to move.

Mr. Sterling approached, looking confused and lost. Words were of little use to a person in his state, but I needed to try and say *something*.

"So sorry for your loss. A horrible tragedy!"

"Thank you...I...need to sit for a moment." He was hardly able to speak.

I felt I might be able to help console him somehow since my husband was killed also. I took a seat near him.

"I haven't formally introduced myself to you," he said. "I'm Lee Sterling."

We shook hands. His felt so cold!

Were my hands any warmer than his? "And I'm Jillian Bradley. Please call me Jillian."

"Thank you," he said. He was on the verge of tears. "How could this happen! I called Birdie last night to say goodnight and everything was fine. Then, Detective McKenzie called early this morning and told me what had happened. "

"It's horrible!" I had to think. How to console him? What to say?

"Who could have done such a thing? The police think my nephew had something to do with it — they've taken him into custody for questioning. But that's impossible! He only met Victoria yesterday."

"She slapped him in front of some of the other guests."

"Yes, I heard about that, too. You must think he was being rude, but trust me — he's not like that. Chase even told us at dinner last night that she apologized and even invited him to a party last night."

"Another one of her parties, huh? That might explain what happened. She's had them before, against our wishes of course. Victoria insists, insisted, on inviting whoever she wanted, whether we approved of them or not."

"That sounds pretty normal for someone of her age. Lee, if there's anything that can be done to help, please tell me."

"Thank you. I don't know if there's anything you can do or not, but it would be nice to have someone to talk to. Birdie, my wife, and I didn't get along very well. But at least she was willing to listen. Now that she's gone...."

Lee began to get emotional. My heart went out to him.

"You can talk to me anytime you like." I placed my hand on his shoulder and then self-consciously removed it. I remembered hearing somewhere that people who put their hands on other people are often perceived as demonstrating power over the person. I didn't want Lee to think that about me!

"My room number is 316 so just call me and leave a message," I said. "We can get a cup of coffee somewhere, and I'd be happy to be a friend right now."

He looked impressed.

"Thanks." He seemed sincere. "I'm going to meet with Reed, that's Dr. Griffin — he's our family physician, before going down to the station. He's going with me to make the identifications. I don't think I could do it alone."

I wrote my room number on my business card and handed it to him. "Please don't hesitate to call me if you want someone to talk to. Besides, I may need your help to get Chase off the hook."

"Is Chase your grandson?"

He must think I'm old. "No, Chase is my nephew and he's a fine young man, not a murderer."

"How can I help? I've never even met him."

"Oh, you'd be surprised. You may know something that you aren't aware of that will help catch the real killer."

"Really?" He looked doubtful. A thought entered my mind. What if *he* was the real killer? Experience had taught me that some people are capable of anything.

"I'll do anything," he said, "Just tell me what to do."

"I will, but right now you'd better go see Dr. Griffin and get through the identifications. I'm glad you're not going by yourself."

"Me, too. Thanks for talking with me. It has helped. I'm sure you'll be hearing from me."

I liked this man.

"See you later. And again, I'm so sorry about your Birdie and Victoria."

Lee closed his eyes. I probably shouldn't have mentioned their names but he eventually nodded.

Without another word, we both entered the elevator and rode in silence.

Cecilia was watching the news when I returned to my room.

Teddy yipped twice when he saw me and wagged his little tail, so happy to see me.

I picked him up gently, gave him a hug, and held him close for a moment. How sad Lee must feel now that his family is gone.

The TV was tuned to a local channel.

"Have you heard the news?" asked Cecilia.

"Yes, unfortunately. The police were wheeling the bodies out of the hotel during our breakfast. They've taken Chase down to the police station." She didn't need to know I gave my card to Lee Sterling.

"Oh no! Chase has been arrested…for what reason? Not the hot tub incident."

"Must be. Somebody must have mentioned it and the police jumped at the chance to put the blame on someone. Of course, we don't believe he did it, but it looks like a motive. We don't know the details yet, but if they find means and opportunity, it will be very difficult to prove he didn't do it."

"What about an alibi?"

"It seems that Chase and the girls were planning to go to a party Victoria was throwing in her suite last night. This morning they're carrying her out in a body bag."

"According to the news, her mother was also killed."

Teddy was glad to be put on his towel.

I sat down next to him on the chair by the sliding door. "It's totally bizarre! I can see maybe one person having an altercation with someone and winding up dead, but two people on the same night…that shows you right there it wasn't Chase."

Cecilia sat on the bed and muted the TV during the commercial. "The news says the police are not giving out any information as to cause of death. Wait, here they are again."

She unmuted the sound.

The same detective who told me I couldn't go with my sister was about to speak.

"We have a person of interest in custody and he's being questioned. That's all I can tell you at the moment. Thank you for your time." He left the platform with reporters following him, their iPhones up in the air trying to record his movements.

"He means Chase, doesn't he?" Cecilia glared.

"I'm afraid so."

She turned to me with that knowing look. "What are you going to do about it, Jillian?"

"Do about it? Me? I don't know yet, but I'll start by going to the pool and see what people are saying. Cecilia, that officer is tough. It won't be easy to get around him."

"But you'll find a way. I know you."

"True. And I've asked the Lord to help me."

"There you go! He knows who killed them."

Cecilia was a believer too. This comforted me.

I looked up as I so often did to pray. "So, Lord, please show me the way. For our family's sake and for Lee's sake, too. Amen."

"Amen...too." Celia smiled.

A horrible thought re-entered my mind.

"Oh, no!" I gasped.

"What is it, Jillian?"

"What if Lee killed them?"

"Lee? Is he a suspect? But why would he kill them?"

"I don't know if he is or not, but husbands are always suspects, aren't they? Why would he kill Victoria?"

"It doesn't make sense, does it?"

"No. This is crazy, but there may have been something going on between his wife and their doctor. They looked a little too cozy together, and men have killed their entire families for their wives cheating on them, just for spite."

She hesitated. "Still...."

My mind shifted to Cecilia's husband Walter, a homicide detective in Clover Hills and a very dear friend of mine.

"Cecilia, I want you to call Walter and have him get all the information on Lee Sterling he can. We have to start somewhere, and truthfully, he would have a motive if his wife had been unfaithful. And have him check out a Dr. Reed Griffin. He's from the San Diego area."

Cecilia wrote down the information and immediately called Walter.

"Hi, sweetheart," she said sweetly, "I miss you, too. Say, have you heard the news yet?"

She looked my way and nodded that he had.

"Sweetheart, they've taken Jillian's nephew into custody as a suspect, and we need to help him. Jillian wants you to check out a *Lee Sterling* and a *Dr. Reed Griffin* for us. They may be suspects in the case — will you do that for us?"

She nodded to me that he would, and I felt a ray of hope that something would turn up to help us get Chase off the hook.

"I love you, too. Talk to you later." She hung up. "He said he'll help us but he'll have to be careful that he doesn't look like he's interfering in a local investigation."

"Understood. You stay with Teddy, and I'll go downstairs and see what I can find out. Let me know the minute Walter finds out anything."

"I will, don't worry. Now get going. Chase won't like jail."

9 Emergency Meeting

I knocked on Mom's door, which was now locked instead of being propped open due to the murders.

"Who is it?" she asked.

"It's me, Jillian. I need to talk to you."

It took a few moments but Mom soon unlocked the door and let me in.

"Jillian, this is awful. Brooke is beside herself worrying about Chase. We must do something!"

"I know, I know." I gave her a brief hug, and we sat down on the sofa in her living room. Her suite was lovely. "All we can do is pray and trust that the Lord will lead us to discover the truth."

"I know, and I do trust Him," she said, even though she still looked worried. "But what are you going to do to help get him out of that awful jail in the meantime?"

"Well, the police will hold him until he can establish an alibi, or until they find another suspect."

I could see the wheels turning in Mom's head with an idea.

"Jillian, we're going to have to call a family meeting and get everyone involved in helping Chase."

"That's probably a very good idea. If we pull together, we may come up with clues the police won't since we've been here the whole time Victoria and her people have. I'll spread the word. When should we meet?"

"The sooner the better, I think." She looked at her watch and then at me. "Let's say noon. We'll tell everyone to bring lunch, and we can put our heads together to see if we can come up with anything."

"Okay, why don't I place an order for everyone, my treat? That should get everyone on board."

"Good idea. I say we order Grilled Chicken Caesars for the adults and pizza for the children."

"Sounds good to me. Let me call right now and set it up." I picked up the phone and placed the order through room service to be delivered in the lobby. "Done!"

"Good. Now I think I'll collapse. This has been quite a strain."

"I think you should, Mom. I'll have Brooke come get you for the meeting and have Greg and Daniel help me with the food."

"What about Will?" She lowered her voice. "You heard Stephanie came to see them yesterday?"

"Yes, I heard, but I didn't hear how it went." I helped her to her bed and covered her with a soft throw, then tucked it under her feet.

"Thank you."

She adjusted her pillow and settled into a comfortable sleeping position. "Suffice it to say, it was an interesting meeting. Will told me he doesn't know what to think."

She looked at me with challenge in her face. "He says she's changed."

I felt the same as she did. I didn't want Will to be hurt again.

"Do you think he still loves her after all this time?" I asked with controlled anxiety.

"It's hard to say. She was his first and only love. They say you never really get over a love like that."

"I can see that. I guess I've never stopped loving my husband...not really. To be honest, though, I still like it when a man pays attention to me. Don't you?"

"Of course! What woman wouldn't? Even at my age."

"What about you? Do you still love Dad?"

Mom was quiet for a moment and then smiled. "I do. When someone lives his whole life just to provide for you and make you happy, you can't help but love him in return the same way."

Her eyes began to close. By the soft smile on her lips, she must have been reminiscing about Dad.

Patting her shoulder, I whispered, "Get some rest. I'll see you in the Cayman Room at noon."

I left and headed to the patio area to look for family members. A few were in Brooke and Greg's room talking about the situation. The air was heavy with desperation.

"Hi," I said, "how is everyone holding up?"

Greg shook his head. "It's not good, Jillian."

"Greg's right," said Will, "the police feel like they have a good motive and evidently Chase was in Victoria's suite all night."

"That's not good, that's not good at all. Do we know what Chase's story is?"

"They say they're keeping everything confidential, Jillian," said Brooke. Her fierce determination to protect her son seemed to have diminished to a state of disbelief and hopelessness. "They won't tell us anything."

"We have to get him a lawyer!"

Greg said, "I've called one. He'll be here this afternoon to go over everything."

"But it sounds like Chase has already told them damaging evidence without having a lawyer present," I said. "Unbelievable that they questioned him without one!"

Now I was mad. "That's how innocent people are convicted, I'm sorry to say."

"Jillian," said Brooke, "what are we going to do? I've heard about people who're arrested for crimes they didn't commit and they're locked up for years! What if Chase...?"

The fear on her face again was unmistakable, and the

truth of what she said made me cringe. I had to be brave for both of us. I walked over and put my arms around her.

"Brooke, it's going to be okay. We know Chase didn't kill those women — we just have to find out who did. Now the first thing we're going to do is think positive." I looked at all of them. "Are you with me?"

Everyone nodded slowly, even Brooke.

"Okay, then. The next thing we're going to do is have an emergency meeting at noon in the Cayman Room. I've ordered pizza and Chicken Caesars — my treat. Every member of the family needs to be there. We're bound to come up with tangible evidence of some kind. We've all seen the Sterlings come and go, who they've been with, things like that."

Daniel spoke up. "I agree with Jillian." Now he sounded enthusiastic. "We've got to do something, and maybe we have seen something that will help the police. Okay, people, let's get our families together and do this thing!"

Brooke seemed to feel more encouraged and smiled just a little.

"You're something else, Jillian, do you know that? And if anyone can find out who did this horrible thing, it's you. Thanks for being here for us. At least now Chase has a chance."

"He has a chance because he didn't do it," I said. "Go wash your face, sister dear, and don't worry. We've got work to do. Just remember, there's a whole passel of Lovejoys to get the job done!"

With a determined spring in my step, I trotted upstairs to tell Cecilia about the meeting.

She was on board to help any way she could.

"We have about thirty minutes before we have to be downstairs. I'll take Teddy for a walk and wait for the food to arrive. Take notes on everything at the meeting. I'll go over it later."

"Right," she said, "I'll go get ready right now. And if

you're wondering, Walter hasn't called yet, but don't worry, I'm sure he will as soon as he finds out anything."

"He will. I'll see you downstairs."

Cecilia waved a quick goodbye as she left.

I was so grateful to have such a dependable assistant and silently thanked God for her help. I attached Teddy's leash to his collar, brushed his fur, and touched up my lipstick.

Teddy seemed to sense the urgency in my spirit by the way he kept looking at me. He was on bouncy alert to assist.

"Let's take a walk."

At the sound of the word, Teddy pricked up his ears and panted — he was excited to go outside again.

Was he thinking of Fancy? I wondered.

Teddy and I returned to the same grassy spot where we met Fancy earlier and paused for Teddy to relieve himself again. Our new friends were not in sight, so we walked back to the hotel and entered through the lobby.

There were several reporters at the desk trying to get information, as well as a couple of guests who didn't look very happy that two homicides had taken place. The manager, doing his best to keep the situation under control, had my sympathy.

I nodded to him briefly, letting him know he still had a faithful guest. He returned the nod with a smile of appreciation at my support.

The delivery person with the salads arrived, and the same pizza delivery guy I met last night came in right behind him. He was moving slow, probably in shock like the rest of us due to the murders.

I signed for the food just as Greg and Daniel arrived to help me. The pizza guy looked at all the food we had to carry down to the Cayman Room.

"Here," he said, "let me help you."

He took all the pizzas and Greg and Daniel grabbed the salads.

I held on to Teddy and led the way to the elevators.

"Thanks for your help," I said.

"No problem. Besides, I wanted to find out if the police nailed that guy who killed Victoria and her mom yet. Do you know anything about it? I mean, you're staying here and all."

The elevator door opened, we all stepped out, and maneuvered toward the Cayman Room.

I slid my room key across the lock and opened the door for the men to carry the food inside. Hungry pairs of eyes greeted us — hungry and apprehensive. I turned to the pizza guy.

"No, I don't think the police have nailed the killer yet. That guy they have in custody happens to be my nephew. *He* did not kill anyone."

"Sorry, ma'am. Just saw the pictures on the news and thought they caught him. Why did they take him in?"

"I'm not at liberty to say. You understand about confidentiality, don't you? It could jeopardize his innocence." I began opening the pizza boxes so the children could start eating.

"Yeah, I understand, but it sure looks like he did it. And no offense, if he did do it, I hope they nail him good. Victoria Sterling didn't deserve to get murdered."

Why is this guy so concerned about Victoria? "Did you know her personally?"

The adults took their salads and began to eat, but I wanted to take advantage of this interview opportunity.

"I'm sorry but I have to go," he said, "my pager is buzzing."

"Of course. Thanks again for your help, Josh."

"Yeah, sure." He left hurriedly.

Why didn't he answer my question?

There was a somber feeling in the room with Chase in custody. My salad wasn't even remotely appetizing.

I took a few bites, then pushed the rest away. Unusual

for me. The police hadn't even started to question anyone besides Chase. Very perplexing, and unfair.

"We're going to get started with our meeting," I began, "Please continue eating your lunches while we talk."

The room grew quiet and all eyes turned toward me.

"This meeting was called because the detective in charge of this investigation wanted nothing to do with any relatives of Chase. But we can't wait any longer to do something since we're only going to be here two more days. I don't know about you, but I plan on Chase leaving with the rest of us."

"We're with you, Jillian," my brothers all said together. Brooke was still an emotional wreck.

"Okay, then. We'll begin. First of all, each one of us may have seen something of importance over the past two days, even if we don't think we have.

"Second, one of you may have seen something that will mean the difference between Chase being convicted or released. I want each one of us to think back to when we first arrived on Saturday and write down everything you remember doing, everyone you saw at the hotel and especially everyone you saw associate with Victoria Sterling's crowd."

"I have paper and pens for everyone," said Cecilia, handing them out to family members.

"Thanks, Cecilia. Everyone, you're free to go about your day, just keep the paper with you and jot down your recollections as they come to you. I'll do the same. Cecilia will compile your notes, so as you think of things, let her know. We don't have much time."

My mom came over, stood next to me, and asked all of us to bow our heads.

"Lord, we pray as a family for You to open our minds and our hearts. Please help us to remember facts that will help us get Chase released. Amen."

Everyone echoed, "Amen."

Brooke raised her hand to speak.

"I want everyone to know I appreciate what you're about to do. However, I don't want this to ruin the reunion that we've worked so hard to attend. Please go on with your plans. I really think it will help to get our brains in gear to help Jillian."

Daniel stood to leave.

"I agree with Brooke. I'm taking Kevin and Sydney boogie boarding if anyone wants to join us."

Samantha, Scott's five-year old daughter, said, "I want to go boogie boarding with Uncle Daniel. Daddy, may I please go?"

Before Scott could answer, Samantha looked at Mallory, who was only three, and said, "You can't go, Mallory, you're too little."

This made us laugh and broke some of the stress we all felt.

Scott had no choice after that. He agreed to let Daniel take Samantha boogie boarding without her little sister.

Ryan, Chase's other brother asked, "Are we still on for the kickball game on the beach?"

"Yeah," said Scott, "I think we should still play. It will keep our spirits up. How about tomorrow morning?"

We agreed on the time, ten o'clock.

"Let's do this, people!" I said, taking a paper and a pen from Cecilia and sitting down at the large table. The salad began to look good to me, so before trying to recollect the past two days, I finished eating. Anyway, my mind worked better when I wasn't hungry.

Cecilia had finished her salad. "Jillian, I'll take Teddy to the room so he can have a nap if you want."

"Thanks. That will leave me free to pick my brain. I'll be up after a while."

"Come on, Teddy," she said, as she took his leash.

"You go and take a nice nap, sweet doggie."

"See you later," she said.

Watching Teddy leave on his leash with Cecilia reminded me of Fancy, leaving with her owner the other day. When was that?

Fancy and her owner...it must have been Sunday afternoon after the photo shoot — between four and six o'clock. I took a pencil and a piece of paper from the table and wrote a note.

Mom came over to me and sat down with her paper and pen in hand. "You know, Victoria and her friends were at the pool the first day we were here."

"That's right — you told me that. Do you remember what they looked like?"

"I think I do. It was Victoria, her friend, a girl in a one-piece bathing suit...."

"The one she's always with...."

"Yes, and then there were two boys. One had dark, curly hair and looked to be about her age, and the other one looked older than the rest of them. He had light brown hair with some sun streaks. It seemed odd to me, but then I'm old...."

"Good job, Mom! Do you think you would recognize them again if you saw them?"

"I think I could."

Mom occasionally couldn't remember things that had currently happened, so this might have been wishful thinking, but those sorts of details could help immensely. One of them could be the face of a killer!

"I'm going to my room now." She began easing herself up for the trip to her room. "Will is coming by to talk about Stephanie. I don't know how it will all work out, but at least I can be a good listener. I'll talk to you later, sweet daughter."

"I love you, Mom. See you later."

My army of sleuths had been launched. Once they got me some leads, I could proceed to find out everyone's alibis. Mom had just given me one — Victoria's friend that she was always with. If Lee called, he might give me her name. That would be, well — perfect!

I jotted down a few more things from the past two days — the crowded lobby when we first arrived, the family with all the children, the arrival of the Victoria Sterling party, Cecilia not feeling well, and family members coming into the lobby to greet me.

The first time I saw Dr. Griffin I'd thought he was Victoria's agent. He must know something about who killed them. Of course, the police would be talking to him if they hadn't by now.

There was something else, something important, but the picture wouldn't form in my mind. All that came to mind was the gift shop, then buying my new outfit and paying for it at the front desk...and then...wait!

Dr. Griffin came into the lobby. He was going somewhere because I asked the concierge about him. She thought I was being nosy. Well, I was — but that's how I operate. Eternal sleuth person. Curious, with a touch of nosy.

There was also a phone call. A guest had a problem of some kind with their room. I couldn't seem to remember what it was exactly, but the concierge had handled it.

Not enough...no...this wasn't going to be easy. But, we would all have to do the best we could.

As the last person to leave the 'Lovejoy Bunker', I didn't mind cleaning up a bit. I threw away the pizza boxes and wiped down the kitchen. Sure, it was housekeeping's job to clean up after guests, but this was a huge mess today. There was no one else for me to take care of. This way, I felt like I was taking care of everyone.

A cup of coffee sounded good, so it was off to the Caribbean Room to get one. As I poured myself a cup, I saw Officer McKenzie taking notes of some kind, sitting at one of the tables talking to Lee. Not stopping to chat, Lee still looked at me as he was being asked questions.

I carried my coffee out to the patio and sat down at a table to take in a few minutes of sun. Ten minutes would give me my daily dose of vitamin D. I closed my eyes, lifted my face upward, and started to enjoy feeling the warmth of the rays, when suddenly, the warmth was gone and coolness replaced it.

A cloud must have passed overhead. I opened my eyes to see Lee standing in front of me. Blushing a little, I turned to see if Officer McKenzie was gone.

Lee seemed to read my mind.

Did Lee see I'm attracted to him? That would be so embarrassing. I sat up straighter in my chair and tried to regain my composure.

Lee pulled out a chair and sat down. "Yeah, he's gone. Have to tell you, he's got a pretty solid case against your nephew."

"Just like that."

"Just like that. According to the officer, your nephew had motive, means and opportunity."

I took a sip of my coffee and observed him carefully. He was so composed. It was hard to read his body language, if he were lying.

"Would you care to share the details?"

"I would if I knew what they were. That detective's not revealing any details until the forensics team is finished and he's talked to everyone involved, but he's convinced your nephew is guilty."

"Are you convinced? After all, it was your wife and daughter. Do you think they could have been murdered by someone they only knew for two days? And did your wife even meet Chase? The charges are absurd, if you ask me."

"What else can I think? We didn't have any enemies, and we've never had any trouble with anyone involved with Victoria in her work. Your nephew, sorry to say, was a sitting duck. It doesn't look good. As to your question, he did meet my wife. She would have been at Victoria's party last night."

"Your wife went to her daughter's parties? Isn't that a little unorthodox?"

He sat back and looked down, gathering his thoughts. He looked up again, straight into my eyes.

"Birdie watched Victoria like a hawk. Besides, my wife liked to drink, so it gave her an excuse." He looked away from me toward the pool. "I used to drink, but lost my taste for it."

"I see."

"Jillian, you'll have to excuse me. There's some business to attend to with the funeral home. Dr. Griffin is going to meet me there in a few minutes and I don't want to keep him waiting."

"Oh, sure, thanks for letting me know about Chase. Perhaps we can talk some more about this later. Lee…you should know that I'm doing everything in my power to find out what really happened."

"We'll talk again. When I get back from making the arrangements, I might call. The hotel has given me a different room."

"Sounds good. Good luck with the arrangements."

Lee left through the Caribbean Room. Making the identifications was going to be tough.

It had been so hard for me not being able to view my husband's body since he died in combat. At the time, my only wish had been to see him one last time. But in retrospect, it was better to remember him as he was before Vietnam.

My cell phone rang. It was Brooke asking me to come to their room. It was only a few steps away to their patio.

Brooke and Greg were waiting for me, alone in the room.

"Come on in, Jillian," said Greg. "Have a seat."

"What's happened?"

I had a feeling the answer was going to be bad.

"They've arrested Chase on suspicion of murdering Victoria Sterling and her mother." His voice was choked with tears. Brooke didn't cry like I thought she would. Either she was in shock, or the mother bear fighting instinct to protect her cubs had kicked in.

"We're going to fight this," she said. Mother bear.

"Yes, we are, and we'll fight until Chase is released. Now, how are you coming with your lists? You haven't had much of a chance, but do you have anything?"

"We have something better," said Greg. His claim had an air of conspiracy about it.

I became instantly curious.

"Chase's lawyer got Chase's side of the story and conveyed it to Brooke and me after talking with him. I think you'll be interested to hear what happened last night."

"I'm all ears."

10 Party Guests

According to Chase, it had been quite a party. There were only seven other guests besides himself, and two of those were his cousins, Lexis and Annika. In addition to loud music and suggestive dancing going on, the alcohol flowed unendingly.

He said everyone, including himself, was taking shots of tequila, followed by swallows of bottled water to keep from getting dehydrated. The pizza delivery guy, fitting the description of the same person who'd delivered to me, stayed after delivering the pizza. Chase was not sure exactly when the guy left the party. Victoria's doctor was also there, sitting alone for most of the night getting drunk on Scotch. That had to have been Reed Griffin.

And then there were three other friends of Victoria's — her girlfriend, by the name of Emily Woods, Victoria's boyfriend of sorts, Tucker Shaw, and another friend whose name Chase didn't catch. The police had taken a statement from all the guests by now, but that didn't mean I couldn't talk to them as well.

A fight over Victoria between Chase and Tucker ended with a broken glass table top, but Chase said neither suffered any injuries.

Chase told the lawyer that Birdie Sterling, Victoria's mother, was also at the party but left around 1:00 a.m. Chase did remember hearing her mom tell Victoria she was heading back to her room and going to bed.

The lawyer said Chase told him he passed out after Victoria's mom left. When he woke up, he saw Emily asleep on the couch in the living room. Everyone else had left. He saw Victoria's door slightly open. She was lying on the bed, fully dressed with her eyes open, staring at the ceiling.

Chase had seen corpses in Iraq and knew immediately Victoria was dead. He said he walked over to her body and took a pulse, confirming what he already knew.

After that, he walked downstairs to the front desk and asked the hotel to call the police. He explained he didn't want to touch anything more than he already had because he knew it would implicate him.

Emily had awakened after Chase did and saw him leave Victoria's room. She told the police that Chase was the last one she saw with Victoria. Poor Chase! No wonder the police believed he did it!

"Brooke," I asked somewhat skeptically, but knew the question was necessary, "how did Victoria die?"

Brooke hung her head with a heaviness any mother would have with the burden of having her son in jail for murder. "She died of a broken neck."

I was stunned. Chase had spoken of learning this skill in his Marine training, and my heart sank. The situation wasn't promising.

"Well, it looks like we'd better start talking to those party guests. One of them must have seen something or someone that stands out as a clue to this whole mess."

Greg stood up. "I agree, but where do we start? I don't think Detective McKenzie is going to like our dabbling in his business, Jillian."

"Who's dabbling? We're simply going to have a few conversations with a few eyewitnesses, and see if we can learn anything that will help Chase get off the hook for a double homicide. By the way, did the lawyer say how

Birdie Sterling was killed?"

Brooke nodded her head. "She was killed the same way Victoria was. Someone broke her neck."

Greg walked over to Brooke and hugged her.

"Don't worry, honey," he said, trying to comfort her, "we know Chase would never kill anyone like that unless they were an enemy of the United States of America. We have to believe that."

"I know, I know," said Brooke, "Jillian, I'm scared. Tell me what to do."

I walked over and sat down beside her on the bed. She was shaking.

I gently put my arm around her shoulders. "Talk to Lexis first, and then to Annika. Get them to tell you everything that happened at the party and write down everything they tell you, okay?"

"Okay." She sighed and stood up slowly. "Just let me freshen my makeup, and I'll go see them right now."

"Good girl," I said, encouraged she was willing to do something to get her mind off worrying.

Greg seemed to be waiting.

"Who do you want me to talk to, Jillian?"

"See if you can strike up a conversation with the good doctor. Get him to open up to you about his relationship with Birdie if you can. Find out how he got along with Victoria and Lee. That's Victoria's father."

"Okay. I'll make mental notes and then come back here and write them down. Now to find him. Wasn't he the one sitting at the photo shoot with Victoria's mother?"

"That's him."

Brooke came into the room after touching up her face.

"Sooner or later everyone passes through the Caribbean Room. I'd watch for him there. You could be there watching TV until he shows up."

Greg picked up his room key and walked to the door.

"I'm going down there right now." He turned to Brooke

and smiled encouragement. "Honey, I'll stay in touch by cell. I love you."

"I love you, too. Good luck!"

"Good luck with Lexis and Annika, too," he said and walked out the door, leaving the two of us together.

Brooke picked up the phone. "I'll call to see if the girls are in their room."

"Good idea. I think I'll track down Emily Woods and see if she'll talk to me. The police told us to stick close to the hotel. She's bound to be on the same floor as me, since that's where Victoria's room was. Let me find out what room she's in."

"Okay. Lexis and Annika aren't answering, so they must be down by the pool. I'll see if I can find them." Brooke picked up a notepad from the table next to the phone. "This should do nicely to take notes on — can't find the piece of paper Cecilia gave me."

"Good luck. I'll see you whenever you finish. I'm anxious to hear what they say."

A small group of hotel workers congregated in the lobby as I started to take the elevator up to the third floor. Standing to one side was Miguel Ramirez. He looked my way. I wanted to find out what the meeting was about — maybe there was something to learn. I walked over, stood next to Miguel, and asked if it was okay for me to listen.

"Sure, Mrs. Bradley," he said, just as the hotel manager addressed the group.

"Now people," he said quietly, "the police have asked everyone who worked last night's shift to give a statement."

There was a buzz among the workers and the manager gestured for quiet. "I have some forms for you to fill out so please come and get one. Fill it out and return it to me as soon as you can. The police need them by the end of the day. You can leave them in my office. Thank you for coming. Now, let's return to work, shall we?"

The group began to disperse, but Miguel lingered.

"I heard they arrested your nephew," he said. "I'm truly sorry. It must be very hard for your family."

"Thank you. Yes, it's been difficult for everyone. We're doing everything we can to prove he's innocent."

"If there is anything, anything at all I can do to help, please let me know. You and your family have been faithful guests for many years, and we would hate for you to stop coming here every year."

"We would hate to stop coming, too. But I don't know how we'll feel if Chase is convicted of a crime he didn't commit.

"Miguel, if you really want to help me, there is something you can do."

"Anything, ma'am. What is it?"

"I need to know who was working last night."

'I'll see what I can do. The last shift is from 3 p.m. to 11 p.m. After that, there's just the night auditor and a security guy until the next morning."

"So there are only two people working during the night?"

"Well, sometimes, if we're really busy, like now, you know, summer time, there is a bellman on call. But usually it's only if there's something special going on."

"Like the party Victoria had last night?"

Miguel nodded.

"There is a copy of the weekly shifts for the housekeepers and maintenance people on the bulletin board in the boiler room downstairs. You can copy the names. I'll go with you so you won't look suspicious."

"Can we go right now?" I was ready.

"Sure. Let me get a form and I'll be right with you. I'll grab you a piece of paper, too."

"Thanks." In order not to be noticed, I waited in the hall for Miguel to join me. He was the last one in line for the forms.

As soon as the manager stepped into his office, Miguel

walked over to me and we took the elevator to the garage.

The boiler room was at the other end of the garage and doubled as a laundry area for housekeeping and guests. No one was inside as Miguel led me to the wall where the shifts were posted. I copied down the names and shifts and placed the paper in a travel brochure I'd picked up by the elevator.

"Thanks, Miguel. This may help. One more thing."

"Sure, ask anything."

"There are six names here besides yours. Would it be possible for me to talk to these people somewhere so I can see if they saw anything that evening? It's really important."

Miguel looked at the concrete floor, thinking.

"What if each one comes to your room, say at different times? Would that work?" He looked again at the list. "Yes, they are all here this afternoon. No one would question it if they carry, say, a cleaning cart or something when they come to your room."

"That should work. I'll be in my room by five o'clock when their shifts begin. I'll order room service, for starters." Miguel looked at me with a touch of amusement in his eyes.

"That would take care of one," he said.

I finally headed upstairs to my room, taking the elevator to the third floor. When I got off, there was yellow crime scene tape draped over what must have been the suite Victoria was staying in down the hall. The room next to it was taped off as well. I had to assume that was Lee and Birdie's room.

A police officer stood guard outside the rooms. A housekeeper was servicing the room on the other side of the suite. I passed Victoria's room and walked past where the housekeeper was working, peering inside to see if anyone was there.

Someone was packing a suitcase on the bed. It was the

same young woman Victoria was always with.

I knocked gently on the door.

"Excuse me, Emily Woods, isn't it?"

"Yes, I'm Emily Woods. What can I do for you? Are you a reporter?"

"No. I'm a friend of Lee Sterling's. My name's Jillian Bradley. I'm a guest here at the hotel."

I didn't mention that I was also Chase's aunt.

"May I come in and talk to you for a few minutes? Are you planning to go home?"

She continued packing. "Yes, as a matter of fact. Look, Mrs. Bradley, I've already talked to the police, and I really don't think I have anything else to say. I'm still very upset, and my parents think I should come home right away."

"Yes, I can understand that. They must be very concerned about you possibly being in the same room as a murderer. If I had a daughter, I would be."

Emily stopped packing and sat down at the edge of the bed. Maybe I'd touched a heartstring of empathy mentioning I didn't have a daughter. I was wrong.

"I'm sorry," she said. "I have a terrible headache. Still feeling hung over from last night."

"I understand."

"Have a seat. I'll tell you what I told the police if that's what you want to know."

"Thanks. Sorry to put you through this again. What I'd really be interested in, and this is to help Lee, of course, is if you can think of anyone who was at that party who had a motive for killing Victoria and her mother."

Emily looked pensive and yet her face was a mask, hiding her true feelings when she spoke.

"I'm still numb, you understand. But I have thought about it, and honestly, Chase Campbell is the only one who could possibly have a motive. Everyone else was Victoria's friend, except for those cousins of Chase. She just invited them to be nice. I don't think they would have a reason to kill them. Not really. And that would just leave Tucker, who loved Victoria...."

"He was her boyfriend?"

"Yeah, and they got along, so why would he kill her?"

"Who else was there?"

"Well, Dr. Griffin was there, but Victoria never had a quarrel with him, if anything she depended on him for...."

"For what, Emily?"

"I'm sorry, Mrs. Bradley. I'd rather not say."

"That's okay."

I could only imagine.

"Was there anyone else that came to the party? Anyone at all?"

Emily stood up from the foot of her bed and walked out onto the balcony.

I followed her, and we both sat down in the two patio chairs.

"There was the pizza guy. He was actually a friend, or I should say acquaintance, who went to high school with us. He got in trouble for harassing Victoria because he kind of stalked her."

"Really? The pizza delivery guy?"

"Yeah. He delivered the pizzas, and then hung around awhile. Victoria wouldn't be mean to him. In fact, she liked the attention because it made Tucker jealous. Just a girl thing. You know."

"Yes, I can see that happening. Victoria was a beautiful girl."

"Yeah, but look where it got her. Murdered." She started to twist the edge of her blouse.

Emily was getting nervous so I decided not to push her too hard.

"Emily, let me treat you to lunch as a way to thank you for talking to me. Would you like that?" For a moment, the mask fell away.

"Yes, that would be nice. Where would we go?"

"Anywhere you like. Let's say tomorrow. Think of a place, give me your cell phone number and address and I'll pick you up."

"No, that's okay. I'll just meet you somewhere. What about Tower 23, you know that new place they just opened?"

"Yes. I've walked past it several times. It looks like a little food for a lot of money."

She looked disappointed.

I continued, "We could go somewhere else if you want."

After more silence, I gave in. "Okay. That's fine. How about noon?"

Emily smiled and nodded.

"Noon it is. And Emily, thanks again for talking with me. I'm sure Lee wants to see justice for his wife and daughter."

"But they've already caught the killer."

"I'm sure if he's guilty, he'll be punished. Let's just say it would be tragic if Chase Campbell were punished for someone else's crimes. Wouldn't you agree?"

"Of course I would."

"Good. I'll see you tomorrow then."

Emily still seemed a bit shocked and probably wasn't able to tell me absolutely everything. Mustn't push too hard, or the memories would stay locked inside her mind.

What time was it? I pulled out my cell phone and checked. Only an hour to go before promising to be in my room for the workers to come and talk to me. Wish I would hear something from other family members! But so far, no one had reported anything. Every moment that nothing happened was a moment closer to Chase being convicted. I prayed for some kind of breakthrough.

When I returned to my room to check in with Teddy and Cecilia, they were both asleep on my bed. Cecilia was just waking up.

"What's this, you two?" I didn't really mind if they had

taken naps or not. "The sea air must be affecting you."

Cecilia sat up and stretched her arms overhead, then stifled a yawn with her hand. "It must be the salt air. Whatever is causing it, I'm totally relaxed. Look at Teddy."

I notice he hadn't even moved since I came into the room.

She smiled lovingly. "He's still in the same position he was when you left."

"And that was right before noon. Well, we'd better wake him and take him for a walk, or he'll wind up wanting to play all night."

"You want me to take him for a walk?" she offered as she slipped on her shoes.

"No, I have a few minutes, so I'll take him. I'm expecting some visitors after five this afternoon."

"Visitors?" She asked rather surprised.

"I have my gardener friend, Miguel, as an ally now. He's sending up members of the staff who were working last night, one at a time, so I can talk to them."

"That's good thinking. I'll wait here so you'll be covered if someone comes. I really don't mind."

"Thanks." I attached Teddy's leash and checked my makeup to see if my lipstick needed any retouching. Just a bit. I had to look presentable in case I ran into Lee.

"I'm sure it won't take me long, but I appreciate it. Okay, we're off."

Normally, there were children running around the hotel dressed in bathing suits and fetching things from their rooms. But now, there was an absence of children running about anywhere. The parents probably felt fearful with a possible murderer on the loose.

A shiver ran down my spine. I happened to believe they were right.

We made it through the boardwalk gate without seeing anyone we needed to talk to sitting at the pool. The weather was overcast and on the chilly side for so late in the afternoon. Out on the ocean, surfers and boogie boarders were wearing wetsuits, so the water must have been cold.

Teddy yipped and drew my attention to a dog tied to a power pole nearby. It was Fancy! I looked around for her owner. He was nowhere in sight.

When Teddy and I approached her, she immediately snarled. I was surprised she didn't remember us, but she was probably afraid of being left by herself, and must have felt naturally defensive.

"It's okay, girl," I said to her softly, "we're not going to harm you."

Fancy was shaking now, and instead of snarling, she tucked her tail between her legs, looking alone and scared. Her owner wasn't anywhere to be seen.

There was really nothing to do, so Teddy and I moved on with our walk, glancing behind us occasionally in hopes her owner would return soon.

Poor Fancy. I hoped that young man didn't leave her alone much longer. Not such a nice owner.

We walked down the boardwalk a little further and then turned around and headed toward the hotel. As we neared the gate, I saw that Fancy was gone. Had someone else taken her?

"Well, Teddy," I said, "let's hope her owner has her now."

Teddy yipped as if to show me he understood what I'd said.

11 Errant Wife

It was surprising to find my brother Will and his ex-wife Stephanie sitting on his private patio by the pool. He hailed me to come over. Upon seeing them together, my feelings were uncertain about the new development. But then, it was really none of my business, except there was a concern that my brother would be hurt again.

I approached the two of them as they sat side-by-side in the iron chairs.

"Hello, Will. Stephanie." My voice was devoid of emotion. "We're surprised to see you again, to say the least. How have you been the past twenty-odd years?"

I immediately regretted my cattiness, but anger welled up for the way she left him with all the responsibility of my nieces. "I apologize," I said, "that was a rude thing to say."

Stephanie shifted in her chair and looked demurely at Will, which to me was disingenuous.

He was affected by her, that was obvious.

"Hello, Jillian. Yes, it has been a long time. I see you still have Teddy."

"Actually, this is about my third Yorkie. I'm surprised you remember."

She smiled at the offhanded compliment.

"Your feelings about me are understandable. I deserve the way you and everyone else feels. Maybe it's too late to apologize for leaving Will and my babies, but I couldn't stay away any longer."

Hearing her refer to my two grown nieces as babies made me cringe, but curiosity stopped me from saying anything.

"So why now? The girls are grown."

"That's exactly the reason. I didn't think Will would even agree to see me before now. But he has, and I'm grateful."

There was some actual sincerity in her voice that, honestly, I had never heard before. But then, I barely knew Stephanie when she and Will married. She left so abruptly after the twins were born, I couldn't say I knew her at all.

Will took her hand, which really made me shiver, and spoke.

"We've had a long talk, and she's seen the girls, Jillian. We've decided to stay in touch."

I felt numb.

"So," I asked, "what do you do now? Do you live in San Diego?"

"Yes, I'm a department manager down at the court house. I've worked my way up since...."

"Since you left?" I finished for her, still feeling defensive for my brother's sake.

"Yes," she said, "since then."

Will withdrew his hand from hers and looked down at the table. I knew he was reliving the hurt he felt when she left.

"To tell you the truth, Jillian, it's actually a relief for me that Stephanie's not dead. I'd thought she was for years."

"But I might as well have been. There hasn't been a day when I didn't think about all of you and what I'd done. But I never had the courage to face up to my leaving. I was so afraid you'd have me arrested for abandonment that I decided to run away and start a new life."

I considered how she might have felt. There was no way I could judge her since I'd never had children. Besides, it wasn't my place to judge anyone, really.

"What are your plans, now that you've reconnected?" I asked in a more civil tone. She looked at Will, as if her answer depended on him, then at me. Her eyes were full of pain.

"No plans, except for wanting to see them one more time."

"And now you've done that." I knew, subconsciously, I wanted her to leave poor Will and his daughters alone.

"Yes, and now I've done that." She got up and started to leave, then turned to Will and extended her hand. "Will, thank you again for being willing to let me have this visit. Maybe one day, you'll be able to forgive me. Hopefully, Lexis and Annika will, too. I know I don't deserve it, but it's still my hope. Goodbye."

She reached out and petted Teddy. He flexed his ears as a sign of liking her. "Hope everything works out for Chase."

"So you know about that?"

"We hear all about things like that at work. I need to be going."

Will had tears in his eyes. Whether it was from the joy at seeing Stephanie again, or from the pain it would bring him, knowing he would never see her again if that were his choice, was uncertain.

"I'll walk you out," he said.

Lexis and Annika walked up behind me after the two left.

"Well, Aunt Jillian," said Lexis, "what do you think of our mom?"

Annika looked sullen and visibly upset.

"It's hard to know what to think. All these years, I've judged your mom harshly for leaving you and your father, but now, I really don't know what to think of her. She sounds sincere, but it's hard to trust someone when they've deserted all of you, like she did."

Annika cut in, "We know what you mean. Lexis and I feel the same way you do. She seems sincere, but since we've never really known her before, it's difficult to know."

"I suppose time will tell," I said. "Have either of you come up with anything you remember about the party last night, or about the Sterlings in general?"

Lexis pulled up a patio chair and sat down. "There was one thing that happened at the party."

"What was that?"

Tucker got a little heated over Victoria. I actually think she enjoyed it. Also, her doctor gave her some kind of pill towards the end of the evening."

"You saw him give her a pill?" This sounded unbelievable. He must have been awfully drunk to be so careless.

"Yep, I sure did. Of course, he was pretty bombed...."

"And we weren't?" asked Annika. "It was just Ecstasy. It's available everywhere. What's the big deal, Lexis?"

"Have either of you used Ecstasy before?" I asked casually, hoping they would tell me they hadn't.

"Of course not, Aunt Jillian," they chimed in together, "but we've been around people who've taken it, and Victoria must have taken it all the time."

Annika seemed quite confident about what she had seen.

"I see. So let me understand. You think Victoria was on Ecstasy and someone murdered her while she was high?"

Lexis said, "That's what we think. But then, why did someone kill her mom? I mean, her mom wasn't even in the room, so someone must have killed Victoria and then left and went to Birdie's room and killed her...."

"Or," said Annika, "someone killed Birdie first and then came into Victoria's room and killed her after that."

"You two are starting to think like me," I said. "But you both have good points. Tell me, did Chase talk to Birdie at the party? Because if he didn't, I don't know if he ever did."

"I never saw him," said Lexis.

"Come to think of it, I never saw him talk to her either."

"So how come the police are so sure Chase did it if he never even spoke to Birdie?" What were they basing their case on anyway? "I think we should talk to Chase's lawyer and tell him what you saw."

"We have, Aunt Jillian," said Annika.

"And they can still hold him? Well, I'll talk to Brooke and Greg and find out if something can be done."

I glanced at the room clock radio. It was five o'clock.

"Oh my, I need to get to my room. Now ladies, if you'll excuse me. Come on Teddy, my love."

I scooped him up and the girls came over and stroked his fur.

"Goodbye, Teddy," said Annika.

"See you later, Aunt Jillian," said Lexis.

"Stay in touch, you two."

Cecilia was talking on the phone as I entered. I assumed she was talking to Walter. I put Teddy in the bathroom and gave him some fresh water, knowing he was probably thirsty after his walk. He lapped thirstily with his tiny tongue, and I was struck by the thought that all living things needed water to live.

All living things…that phrase made me wonder about the living thing that killed a mother and her daughter. This was such a strange case. I'd heard of murderers raping and killing mothers and daughters, even in front of their husbands and fathers, but for someone to take a chance and murder someone in a public hotel like this would require pre-meditation.

The killer *must* have some history with the Sterling family, and the sooner we found the link, the sooner we would find the killer.

There was a knock on my door. Cecilia and I became alert.

"Housekeeping," a woman's voice announced. Cecilia got the door since I was putting Teddy on his towel at the foot of my bed.

"Please come in," she said. A matronly woman dressed in a hotel uniform entered. She looked nervous as she left her cart in the hallway and closed the door behind her.

"Miguel said I should come and talk to you about...you know."

Cecilia offered her a chair. "Please sit down."

She sat reluctantly.

Cecilia excused herself so the woman would feel more comfortable in talking with me.

"Thank you so much for coming, it's much appreciated. I'm Jillian Bradley." I offered my hand in friendship.

She took it but her grip was weak.

"Connie. What would you like to know?" Her eyes did not meet mine, and there was a sense of distrust. Her body language told me she was apprehensive in coming to see me — she fidgeted with her hands and looked away when I spoke.

"First of all," I said, "You need to know that the police have arrested my nephew for the murders."

I let this sink in and waited for her reaction.

"I'm so sorry, Mrs. Bradley. That must be awful for your family."

"It is, Connie. You also need to know that we believe he's innocent — he was just in the wrong place at the wrong time. But unless we find out who really killed those poor women, my nephew will be locked away, perhaps for life. You can see that, can't you?"

"Yes, ma'am. I'll tell you what I saw."

"Thank you, Connie. Just start at the beginning. I'm going to write down what you say so I can compare notes with the others, if that's okay with you."

"Sure, I suppose it will be okay. But what if I say something that will get me in trouble?"

"I'll leave your name out of this, if you want me to. But if you tell me something the police need to convict the real killer, you may have to testify. I'll tell you what. Let's not worry about that right now. We have to think about saving an innocent young man."

"But I have to think about protecting myself, Mrs. Bradley. I have two children and a husband who is out of work right now. They depend on me. I *have* to think of them first."

This was not going to be easy. I sighed, but fully understood where she was coming from.

"Let's just do the best we can. If you don't want me to mention you, I won't. But I'd rather know what happened and not be able to prove it, than to not know at all and watch my nephew get convicted without even trying to catch the person who did it."

"You're right. Like you say, let's just do the best we can."

"What time did you start your shift?"

"Three o'clock. I got off at eleven."

"And what are your duties during that time? Surely you don't service the rooms."

"We do the laundry, and we're on call in case a guest should need anything."

"And did anyone in Victoria's suite need anything that night?"

"There was a call for a cleanup. I think someone accidentally broke the glass top on the table in the living room."

"What time was this?"

"It was around ten-thirty."

"Did you go on the call?"

"Yes, I went with Lucas."

"And together, you cleaned up the mess."

"Yes."

"Tell me about it."

"Well, Lucas and I knocked on the door and said, "Housekeeping," like we always do. There was loud music going on so we had to say it several times. Finally, a young woman...."

"What did she look like?"

"She had reddish-blond hair. She wasn't like Victoria at all."

I wrote down the name of Emily Woods.

"Please go on, what happened when you went inside?"

"Like I was saying, there was loud music, and people were dancing and laughing and drinking, of course. There were many liquor bottles everywhere. I thought about my poor friend who would have to clean up the room in the morning."

"How many people were there? Can you remember?"

"Let me think. I remember Victoria and her mother, of course. Her mother was sitting with that doctor who's always with them. And I remember the girl who answered the door."

"That's Emily Woods, I'm pretty sure."

"And, let me see, there were two pretty girls, one with dark hair and the other with light brown hair who were talking with the blond man."

"That was my nephew and my two nieces, I think."

"And I recognized the pizza delivery guy, too. He was there, and I thought it strange that he stayed."

"Is that everyone you saw?"

Connie stopped and put her head down, trying to remember.

"There was only one other young man. He was dancing with Victoria and they looked sweet on each other."

"Tucker Shaw," I murmured. "So then what happened?"

"Lucas picked up the large pieces of broken glass and put them outside the door. I vacuumed up the rest and I cleaned away some of the trash that had piled up. Lucas went to get a new table top. This wasn't the first time

NANCY JILL THAMES

something like this has happened.

"And then?"

"And then I left."

"So you weren't there when Lucas brought the new table top."

"No, I went to the office to fold laundry. This morning, when I got off work, I saw the police all over the place and I heard about the murders.

"It's eerie, Mrs. Bradley, to come to work again where someone's been murdered. I really need to go start my shift now. I hope I've been of some help. And good luck to your nephew."

"Thanks, Connie. You've been very helpful. If you see someone who worked last night, please tell them to come and talk to me, won't you?"

"I will. You're a nice lady, Mrs. Bradley. And your dog is well-behaved, too."

Teddy woofed.

He needed his supper, so I prepared the groceries I'd bought from a market down the street. I made a meal of turkey breast, mixed veggies, a little brown rice, and a teeny bit of canned fruit and a sprinkle of cheese, adding a small cup of milk and more fresh water next to his feeding dish.

"Teddy? Supper!"

He bounded off the bed and pranced into the bathroom, his ears pricked up at hearing his name and the word supper.

Better order my own.

There was another knock on my door. Another staff member? When I opened the door, my brother, Will stood there. He looked tired and troubled.

"Will? Come in. What's going on? Here, come and sit down."

He plopped down in the chair and let out a long sigh.

"What am I going to do about Stephanie, Jillian? You're

108

a problem-solver. What would you do if you were me?"

Pausing before saying my first thought, which was negative, I tried seeing the situation from his point of view.

"Well, for starters, I'm not you. Have you had dinner yet? I'm just about ready to order some."

"Thanks, you go ahead, I'm not really hungry."

"Hmm." I picked up the phone and ordered from the Firehouse Pub menu: pan-roasted halibut with cherry tomatoes, asparagus & shiitake mushrooms topped with a citrus butter sauce served over garlic-mashed potatoes.

"You know I only eat half of everything to keep my weight off, don't you?"

Will was lost in thought but finally looked up at me.

"No, I didn't know that. Thanks for the offer."

It was clear what Will wanted me to say, but what *wasn't* clear was if what he wanted and what he needed were the same.

"Will, what does Stephanie want from you and the girls? Has she told you?"

"We've talked, yes. Jillian, she's kept up with us all these years. Don't know how she did it, but she's been on the outside looking in this whole time! How can I think she doesn't care if that's true?"

"There's really no way to know. Will, you're going to have to go with your gut feeling on this one. Try to imagine what your life was like after she left you and compare that to what it could be if she were back in your lives. You should ask yourself if you could stand the pain if she returns and then leaves again."

He began to pace.

"After she left, it was if the wind had been knocked out of me. That feeling lasted for years. It was only after sending the girls away to boarding school and getting caught up in my work that I even felt halfway normal again."

"So, what would change if you asked her to be part of

NANCY JILL THAMES

your life again?"

He sighed and covered his mouth with his left hand, seeming to think hard about my question. He clasped his hands behind his neck and stretched to relieve the tension.

"I think I would be happy again. I haven't been happy since she left."

"Then that's your answer. You may want to go slow at first, to make sure it's real. It will take quite a bit of adjustment. But the main thing you're going to have to do is forgive her. Do you think you can do that?"

"That's the hard part. I want to, I really do. But right now, there has to be proof from her that she's matured and won't run away again if things get too tough."

"That's something you'll have to work on together. What's your next move?"

"She gave me her phone number and address and told me she wouldn't contact me again unless I called her. Jillian, my heart tells me I've never stopped loving her, but my mind tells me I might get burned again. Maybe I should stay away from the flame."

"Don't you think it depends on what flame you're talking about? It seems to me you still have the flame of love burning, but there's also the flame of her desertion that burned you quite badly. Looks like you have a tough choice with only a fifty-fifty chance of success either way."

"That's what I think, too."

I heard someone knock on the door and went to answer it as I tossed a comment over my shoulder.

"What you need is to sleep on it, dear brother."

12 A Good Omen

The next person on staff I talked to was the young girl who had just brought me room service. She was small and not unattractive. Her smile was forced, but I understood under the circumstances.

"Where would you like me to sit the tray?" She looked around the room.

"Just put it on the desk. That will be fine."

She sat the tray on the desk carefully and handed me the bill to sign. I took my time.

"I see your name is Rose. That's my middle name."

"Really? It's not very common. You're only the second person I know who has it."

"My name is Jillian Rose Bradley. It's nice to meet you. This is my brother, Will Lovejoy."

"Hi, Rose," he said rather distractedly. I knew he was still thinking about Stephanie.

"Were you working this shift last night?" I asked.

"You mean when the murders happened?" The blood drained from her small face. "Yes, I was. But I didn't see or hear anything. I never went inside those rooms."

"Lucky for you," said Will. He walked over to the desk and lifted the metal cover off the entrée. "This looks amazing, Jillian. Think I will have half."

"Please help yourself."

I signed the bill and thanked Rose for delivering it. She

started to leave.

"Rose, just a moment. Who does the staff say killed those women?"

She paused and then looked me in the eye. "All I can tell you is everyone thinks the murderer is still with us."

"Why do they think that? You know they've made an arrest."

"I can't explain it. It's just a feeling in the air."

Will used a spoon to begin eating the halibut.

"So what you're saying is that the staff isn't feeling relieved just because they've arrested someone, is that it?"

"Yes," she said. "Something, like a feeling of evil, is still here. I'm sorry — I really have to return to my duties."

She walked out of the room and quietly closed the door behind her.

I went over to the desk to rescue what was left of my dinner. Will had helped himself to more than half, but I didn't mind. The portions were huge. I sat on the bed with Teddy lying beside me. He wanted a few morsels of my dinner, so I gave him a few tiny bites.

"Well, what do you make of what Rose said?" I asked as I took the first bite. It was delicious.

"I'd say it was a good omen that Chase is innocent."

"Yes, but feelings are one thing — what we need is proof that someone else did it."

"Jillian, I know how your brain works. Usually overtime."

He knew me well — it was true.

"Why don't you finish your dinner and relax a minute," he said. "It will do you good. This food is great, by the way. Good choice."

Will was right, but I couldn't rest knowing there was still someone out there getting away with killing those two poor women. Lee...it probably hadn't even really hit him yet that they were gone. He hadn't called. Probably had a million things to do. He may *never* call me.

After we finished our meal, I phoned to have someone come and get the tray.

"I think I'll go to my room," he said, "if you don't mind being alone."

Then he shook his head, embarrassed. "Sorry I said that."

"It's okay — you're only thinking of me. Besides, I'm used to being alone. It's not all that bad. But what about you? Do you ever feel unbearably lonely?"

"At times. But I stay busy with my work, and I play computer games. In a way they make me feel connected."

"To other people?"

"Yes, something like that. See you in the morning. You're an early riser like me, aren't you?"

"Sure am. Be down about 7 a.m. I always get dressed first thing so I'm ready for the day."

"See you then. Goodnight. Goodnight, Teddy. Guard your mistress well."

Until Will said that, I never thought I might need guarding.

I only hoped that wouldn't prove true.

Will placed the tray outside my door for me and went downstairs.

Just as I began to get ready for bed, the phone rang. It caught me by surprise. It was Lee.

When I asked him about his day, he told me about all the calls he'd had to field. Calls from Victoria's work, calls from the police, calls from people with condolences. He was exhausted but wound up at the same time.

Lee began to cry and apologized right away. He told me how utterly alone he felt, and I told him I understood. He said the hotel had given him another room so the police could do the forensics. Listening to him talk, it sounded like he was still in shock.

He asked me to meet him down by the pool where we could talk. It was nice not asking me to his room, or suggesting he come to mine.

I explained that I must stay in my room in case a staff member wanted to talk about last night. He said he understood and said he just didn't want to be alone. We talked some more about Birdie, how they met, the difficult first years they had together.

But weren't everyone's first years of marriage difficult? He wanted to talk about Birdie, and I asked how she got her name. He said everyone asked that question, but he never got tired of telling the story about how she was the lead in the musical "Bye Bye Birdie" in high school. After that, everyone called her Birdie and the name stuck.

When he talked about Victoria, I learned they had moved to L.A. when she was just a little girl. Birdie was the one who nurtured Victoria's acting career — it was never really Victoria's idea to get into the acting business.

He knew all along that it had been his wife's unfulfilled dream, but he said as long as it made her happy, it didn't matter what she did.

It's important to let a bereaved person talk all they want about the person they had lost. As I listened, it seemed Lee loved Birdie as much as any man could.

Soon, he apologized for talking about her so much, but I assured him it was the best thing he could do right now.

In discussing his business, trying to get him to start thinking about the future, all he told me was that he was a regional manager for a computer firm. That must have been why he traveled so much.

Lee asked if I had learned anything more. I told him about the fight between Chase and Tucker, how the glass tabletop got broken and some staffers had to come and clean up the mess. He said he wasn't surprised about the fight. Boys were always fighting over Victoria.

When I mentioned what Rose said about the staff feeling that the murderer was still present, he was quiet for a moment. I asked what he was thinking. He told me he was trying to picture Tucker killing Victoria and Birdie, but the image wouldn't come. Birdie liked Tucker, he told me, and thought he was a nice choice for Victoria.

"Did you like him?" I asked.

He said he had no feelings either way. He barely saw them together because he was traveling on business most of the time.

There was still the question of whether or not Birdie kept company with Dr. Griffin while Lee was away. I asked what he thought of Dr. Griffin, whether he could have killed like that.

Lee paused for just a second, and then said he had no reason to think so. I asked for Tucker Shaw's phone number and Dr. Griffin's as well. He left the phone for a moment and then gave me the information.

It was good to let Lee talk all he wanted, knowing how much it helped when you lost a mate. When my husband died in Vietnam, as many of my friends did, I was surrounded with people who supported me until I asked them to leave me for a while so I could get some rest.

I wondered if Lee had any friends like that since he had chosen to call me, practically a stranger.

We finally said goodnight and promised to touch base tomorrow. I invited him to our family's kickball game on the beach, but he politely declined.

I suggested having tea tomorrow afternoon at The Mad Dog Café. He agreed, thanked me for listening and we ended the call.

Teddy stretched out his paws and then his back legs, letting me know it was time to go to bed. He pricked up his ears, jumped down off the bed and went over to where his toys were. He selected one of his favorites and set it at my feet for a game of fetch. This sweet little dog needed more attention than I had been giving him with my mind on the murders.

"Okay, precious doggie." I tugged at the little blue

stuffed pig, trying to wrestle it away.

Teddy growled ferociously, trying to hold on to it. I finally pulled it out of his mouth and threw the little pig across the room. "Fetch!" I commanded. Teddy bounded after it, picked it up in his tiny mouth and raced back, dropping the pig at my feet for me to throw again. We did this about four times until Teddy was panting. He walked over to his leash, telling me he needed to go outside one more time before bed.

Cecilia had volunteered to take him for a walk in case another staff member came to see me. I rang her, and as always, Cecilia cheerfully said she was happy to. She was knocking on my door within two minutes.

"You look awfully tired. Any luck tonight?" She walked over and put the leash on Teddy. It *had* been a long day.

"Well," I replied, "if you count a broken glass table top, a fight between Chase and Tucker Shaw, and spooky feelings the staff are having about the murderer still being on the premises, I guess you could call that luck. Anyway, Lee called me."

"He did? What did you talk about, Jillian, if you don't mind me asking?"

"This and that. He's just lost his wife and daughter, so he needed someone to listen. No one can understand that unless they've been through it like I have, believe me."

"It's probably much worse than when I lost Mom. Dad took it hard, as you well remember."

"Hard enough to risk losing his life in that laboratory."

"At least he's okay now with Daisy to keep him company. I really like her."

"Me, too. Wish she were here to help us find the killer. She really has audacity, doesn't she?"

"Yes, and she took good care of me when I was so weak, too."

"Have you heard from Walter yet on that information I asked you for?"

"He hasn't had a chance yet. The department is keeping him busy day and night. He'll never say no — you know him."

"Hmm. He's a machine when it comes to his work. How have you been feeling, by the way? I've been so busy that I haven't had a chance to ask."

"I'm fine. As long as I don't let myself get too hungry, there doesn't seem to be any problem."

Teddy walked to the door dragging his leash. We laughed at him trying to tell us Cecilia had better hurry with his walk.

"I'll see you in a few minutes, Jillian. Come on, Teddy. Let's go."

After they left, I checked the time. It was late — nearly ten-thirty. None of the news channels had any coverage of Chase. Nothing. That meant the police were holding their cards close to their chest.

Fine. Our family would be passing our cards around to find a good hand. We would see what happened.

It was after eleven — no one else was going to show up. I looked at the list Miguel had made for me and saw four other names. One was Lucas Kasner — the one Connie said brought the tabletop up from the storeroom. The security guard that night was a man named Marc Yeager, and the two other housekeepers were Theresa Gillis and Martina Williams. There was no bellman listed. Maybe he wasn't on the schedule because he was added at the last minute. I would have to check.

So exhausted!

Cecilia dropped off Teddy from his walk. He went straight to the bathroom for a last drink of water, then looked at me with his head cocked to one side, as if to say, "I'm tired too, Mistress. Please put me to bed."

I picked him up, sat him on his towel, stroked his fur and told him what a good dog he was. I thought of Fancy and wondered where she was sleeping tonight.

"You're one lucky little dog, Teddy. Fancy may be sleeping outside, for all we know."

When I said Fancy, Teddy's ears popped up in recognition. "Now, now, don't think about her. Just lie down and go to sleep while I take my bath."

I filled the tub with hot water and added shampoo for bubbles. After removing my makeup while the tub filled, I climbed slowly into the lovely bath and sank up to my neck beneath the soothing water. My tiredness melted away. I tried to clear my mind of worry over Chase and focus on answers.

The image came of Victoria at her party: a pretty starlet who loved attention, especially of the male variety.

I pictured the boys who were there — Chase, Tucker, Dr. Griffin (although he was certainly no boy), Josh the pizza guy and...there was one other. The one Chase said he saw but never met. Someone must know who he was. I bet Emily did. I would definitely ask her when we had lunch tomorrow.

After drying off and putting on my new silk pajamas bought as a treat for the trip, I sprayed myself with my Legacy perfume. Climbing beneath the cool clean sheets was heavenly.

Sleep....

Instead, I saw an image of a man's back leaning over Victoria and choking the life out of her. My eyes popped wide open. Right, the killer couldn't have choked her without someone in the next room hearing her struggle. That would mean whoever killed her did it swiftly, quietly, and then walked away, right past two people who were asleep.

Emily and Chase.

If it did happen that way, whoever it was must have entered the room after everyone left and after Emily and Chase were asleep. How would someone know that?

Unless they were listening outside at the door until

everything was quiet when they could assume that everyone was sleeping. It was possible.

Several times, when I babysat for my nieces and nephews on occasion, I'd put them down for a nap, close the door and let them cry for a while. And then, just like the killer must have done, I would listen until the crying stopped and the room was quiet. After a moment, I opened the door slowly and checked to see if the baby was asleep.

Did the killer do just that? Wait until it was quiet and then open the door slowly to see if everyone was asleep before coming in and killing Victoria? It could have happened that way.

And what did he or she do next? Slip out the door, walk next door to Birdie's room, listen again, open the door, go in and kill her, too? If it did happen that way, all they would have to do would be to leave the premises inconspicuously and no one would have any idea what they'd done.

My eyes started to grow heavy. Sleep was finally coming as my body started to relax. I forced myself to remember my thoughts by repeating the word hallways three times.

Tomorrow I would focus on finding out who was in the hallways at the time of the murders, and where they went afterward. Hallways... hallways...hallways.

I finally drifted off to sleep.

13 Kickball on the Beach

The dream began to slowly fade. I didn't want to wake up until it ended. Different people were taking turns choking Victoria, but all I could see were their backs.

Then the dream changed and Victoria's face became Birdie's face and she smiled at me. Why wouldn't the killer turn around and look at me? Then I would know who it was.

Eventually, the dream had to end, and it frustrated me… still no clue to the murderer's identity.

I gasped in utter disappointment as consciousness intruded. It was time to wake up. Remembering the tasks before me today, my mood lightened.

I stretched my arms overhead to get the blood flowing. Teddy woke, yawned, and stretched his paws out in front of him. He then repeated the stretching with his hind legs.

"Good morning, sweet doggie. I bet you'd like to go for a walk, wouldn't you?" Teddy's ears were at full salute at the mention of a walk. "Give me a minute. You can wait, can't you?"

He plopped back down on the towel and relaxed.

"I'll take that as a yes."

Donning a white knife-pleated skirt, black tank, and two shell necklaces, I stepped out with Teddy to Cecilia's room to see what she'd like to do for breakfast.

"Come on in," she said. She was dressed and seemed

quite awake. Her computer was on and I was curious. "What have you been doing so early this morning? Working on an article?"

She followed my gaze and nodded. "It's an editorial discussing the pros and cons of using drug sniffing dogs on high school campuses."

"So it's coming to that?"

"I'm afraid so. They probably should have used them when I was in high school. Maybe there wouldn't be so many people on drugs nowadays if they had."

"You might be right. How about some breakfast?"

Teddy yipped.

"Okay, you'd like some, but I was asking Cecilia," I said.

"Sure. Where sounds good? You know Pacific Beach better than I do."

"Well, actually, why don't we just go downstairs and eat here? I have a lot to do."

"That's fine with me. I have work, too. I'm ready whenever you are."

"Let me put Teddy in his tote and I'll meet you at the elevator."

"Okay. See you in a minute."

After stuffing Teddy in his tote, promising to take him for a short walk before we ate, the three of us descended in the elevator and walked to the Caribbean Room where we found quite a crowd. I noticed a few reporters and felt they were intruding.

Cecilia must have noticed how I felt because she smiled and reminded me that she was a reporter, too. "Maybe the crowd will thin out by the time we return from Teddy's walk."

"Let's go, Teddy. Cecilia's probably right."

It was good to have Cecilia come with us, since she hadn't been out of the hotel. And even though it was still early, there were a lot of people taking walks like we were.

Others were jogging on the beach below. Teddy chose a spot, and we paused to inhale some of the ocean air. The sky was overcast again, reminding me that Chase had a black cloud covering him, too.

Casually glancing around to see if I could see Fancy anywhere, I couldn't find her. She wasn't chained up anymore, and hopefully she was with her owner. Someone could have taken her, though. Poor dog.

When we came in through the gate, Miguel was tending the plants. Another staff member was hosing down the pavement around the pool again. We both smiled and Miguel nodded and said good morning. It might have been my imagination, but it seemed like he wanted to talk to me.

"Cecilia, why don't you go on ahead — be there in just a minute. I want to talk to Miguel."

"Sure, Jillian. Would you like for me to take Teddy?"

"No, he can stay with me."

She left me to check in with Miguel.

He walked around the corner, out of sight, and I followed him as casually as I could so we wouldn't attract any attention. When I caught up to where he was tidying up a flowerbed, deadheading some impatiens, he smiled and continued working.

"Did anyone come to your room last night, Mrs. Bradley?" he asked softly.

"Yes. Connie and Rose. They were the only ones who were brave enough, I suppose."

"You were lucky that even they came. The staff is worried that the killer is still here. No one is even talking about what happened for fear they might put themselves in danger."

"That's understandable. By the way, I saw one of the servers with a name tag that had your same last name. Was that the son you mentioned who works here?"

"Yes, that's him," he said.

I could tell he was very proud of his son.

"Most young people don't appreciate old ladies like me fussing over them...."

"You are not an old lady, Mrs. Bradley."

"Well, thank you, Miguel, but I'm old enough to be a senior citizen!"

"Never would have thought it, ma'am." He looked around and must have seen the other workers watching us. "I'd better stop talking and get to work."

"Good idea." Using a louder voice, I said, "the grounds are looking just lovely, Miguel, just lovely!"

"Thank you, ma'am," he said, playing along.

Walking inside to get in line for the buffet, I passed Cecilia sitting by herself on the patio talking on her phone, probably to Walter.

By this time, many of my family were down for breakfast. After I'd selected my food, my mom ushered me over to sit with her.

"Good morning," she greeted me in a perky voice.

Hugs followed. She scooted over to make room. I took the food off my tray and placed it on the table.

"Did you sleep well?" I asked, knowing that at her age, it was an ongoing issue.

She shrugged uncomfortably, so evidently, she hadn't.

I took a sip of the delicious coffee.

"No, I didn't. But I'm not the only one. Everyone I've talked to this morning had trouble sleeping with this murder going on. Brooke looks awful. She's been crying, you can tell, even though she's trying to put up a brave front."

"Well, what we need is a diversion. If we cleared our minds, you know, gave them a rest, we all may remember something that happened. Ryan's in charge of the kickball game today. Thought I heard ten."

"That's the time I heard. I may go for a short walk before the game starts. I'll need to be loosened up."

"Mom, you're amazing, did you know that? How many

eighty-seven-year-old women do you know that get out there and play kickball?"

"Not very many, I guess. At least I'll have a runner. I've asked Kevin and he said he would. You should have seen his face when I asked. It was as if he'd been given a serious assignment. Kaitlin told me he thought I picked him because he could run the fastest."

"That's so cute!"

We drank more coffee and chatted about plans for the day. I told her I was having lunch with Emily Woods but decided not to mention my tea meeting with Lee that afternoon. My family probably wouldn't understand right now.

Teddy let out a teeny whimper, reminding me that I'd promised him some morsels of breakfast. The hotel had said that if he stayed in his tote, he could come inside the Caribbean Room for breakfast. As I hand fed him some small bites of scrambled egg, bacon, pastry and orange, Mom watched and smiled.

"Jillian, I can't believe the way you baby that dog!"

"Mom, he's my companion. He gives me someone to take care of."

"Well, I *don't* have a companion, and I sure don't need someone to take care of."

"You're really sensitive about this, aren't you? Mom, you deserve to be able to enjoy your freedom now after raising us children. But remember, you had a husband and three children to keep you occupied all those years. As a widow with no children, I would have been alone and terribly bored."

"I'm sorry. Sometimes it gets tiresome having people telling me what they think I need all the time. I was really only teasing you. Teddy is a wonderful little dog and he's good company for you. Are you bringing him to the game?"

"No, I really wanted to. He would enjoy the beach, but

there are time restrictions during the day."

"He would enjoy the beach? I didn't think dogs enjoyed anything."

"Haven't you ever seen a dog with a big juicy bone?"

"Point taken. I'm going for that walk now. Ten o'clock will be here before you know it."

"See you then."

She slowly extricated herself from the cozy booth, stood, got her bearings, and then headed to her room to prepare for her walk.

Kaitlin got Silas out of his high chair and moved away from the table covered with Fruit Loops, half-eaten pastries, and crumpled napkins, several of which looked like they'd been used to sop up spilled milk. She walked over to where I was sitting.

"Where are Kevin and Sydney?" I asked.

Silas gave me a huge smile, and it thrilled me that he liked me.

"They're with Grandma getting ready for the beach. Kevin's Grandmother Lovejoy's runner. He's really excited."

"So I heard. I'm going to get a runner, too. My base tagging days are over, I'm afraid."

"Maybe," she laughed, "but you can still kick pretty well, Aunt Jillian." The compliment made me smile.

"I'll see you down there in a little while."

Scott, my nephew, and his wife Rachel came in with Samantha and Mallory to have breakfast. They looked around for a place to sit. The hotel got more crowded every year due to its popularity for family reunions. I decided now was a good time to leave so I stood and offered my table to them.

"Are you sure, Aunt Jillian?" asked Rachel.

She was trying to keep Mallory from pulling Samantha's hair.

"Girls, stop it!"

She sat them opposite to each other so they wouldn't fight.

"Sorry, they're just trying to get attention."

"Well, you'd better give it to them. Teddy and I need to go to the room and get ready for the game. You're coming, aren't you?"

"Of course!"

I had an idea.

I looked at Samantha and asked, "Would you like to be my runner today?"

She timidly nodded her head yes.

"Thank you, sweetheart. You can run fast, can't you?"

She giggled at the attention and Rachel silently mouthed the words, "thank you."

Cecilia came in from the patio, beaming. It was obvious she had been talking to Walter. Those two had been in love since they worked together at The Ritz-Carlton in Half Moon Bay years ago — they just hadn't realized it until Cecilia and I were in Scottsdale a few years later. Walter had ended a relationship because deep down, he knew Cecilia was really the one he loved.

"Walter says 'hi'."

"I'm sure you miss him."

"And before you ask, he did a background check on Lee Sterling and Dr. Griffin. Everything checked out normal with Lee but there were a few red flags with Dr. Griffin. He's had complaints filed against him from patients. I'll do some more digging."

Hearing the news about Lee was a relief. As far as I was concerned, Dr. Griffin made a good suspect.

"Next time you talk to him please let him know I appreciate him checking. Cecilia, would you please make arrangements with the desk to have two beach chairs sent down for Mother and me? I know she'd appreciate it.

"I'll need you to watch Teddy during the game. Dogs aren't allowed on the beach from nine to six. Also, while you're there, please have them print off an American flag. We'll need one for the national anthem."

"Seriously? Never mind, I'll do it right now. I'll see you later. Just give me a knock when you're ready for me to watch Teddy. He's welcome to stay with me in my room."

"Thanks, dear."

After getting Teddy situated with Cecilia I went to change into my black crop sweats and yellow and white striped top — a perfect outfit to wear for playing kickball.

Walking down the long winding wooden staircase to the beach was not difficult — climbing back up was the problem. Mustn't think about that right now.

Beach goers going up and down the stairs passed by me, some with surfboards, others with children holding sand pails full of scoops and shovels.

Me? I was the one loaded with two beach chairs and a beach bag.

After what seemed like an eternity of steps, I finally reached the beach and stepped into the soft sand, which oozed over my sandals and caused resistance as I tried to walk. Members of my family were up ahead.

Ryan and Scott were throwing practice balls for Rachel and Christina. Brooke and Paige were standing guard over Paxton and Silas, holding them, while Kaitlin, Lexis and Annika took Sydney and Samantha for a little swim. Kevin and Mallory were busy digging in the sand with pails and shovels.

Kevin took a pail and filled it with ocean water so he and Mallory could mix it with sand and make mud forms to build a sandcastle.

Seagulls screeched overhead as I set up the chairs and offered one to Mother. She was grateful for my consideration of her comfort.

Greg made the team assignments, and for some reason, my brothers didn't want Grandmother or me on theirs. Couldn't imagine why not.

After the athletes in the group settled the team choices, I pulled out the paper flag and asked Will to lead in a prayer for safety. Then we recited the Pledge of Allegiance and joined in singing the National Anthem.

By this time, a crowd had formed on the precipice overhead watching the spectacle. I looked up and thought there was a familiar face.

"Mother, isn't that Dr. Griffin up there watching us?"

She turned to follow my gaze and then turned to me.

"You might be right."

It didn't seem important until Mother took a second look.

"Jillian, do you see that young man who just walked up to him? The one with the dog?"

It was Fancy, wagging her tail, standing next to her master!

"Yes, I ran across them when I took Teddy for a walk yesterday."

Mom raised her eyebrows.

"That young man was with Victoria at the pool the first day we were here. Remember me telling you she was with two boys?"

"Are you sure it's the same guy? It's a little far to see."

"You're sure that it's Dr. Griffin, aren't you?"

"Yes."

"Well, since I've had my cataract surgery my vision is perfect, and I'm telling you that that young man was with Victoria at the pool."

Mother was not going to relent, so I chose to accept what she saw.

"Sorry, Mother. I believe you. He must know them somehow."

"I'm sure you'll figure out how, knowing you."

"Let's play ball," said Greg. The game began.

First up to kick was Lexis. The outfielders took a step back. She felt empowered with their perception of her strength and prepared to kick as the pitch came toward her. She kicked, and the ball hurled into the air right between the pitcher and second base.

Cheers and applause broke out as Lexis ran toward first base.

But wait! Greg raced to second base, trying to catch the ball before Lexis could score. He dived into the air, stretched out his arms and grabbed the ball. Lexis had almost reached first base when Greg did a somersault on the sand. We looked, and as he turned over, we saw that he was clutching the ball to his chest. Lexis was out! Cheers rang out from Greg's team. Sympathy hugs and pats commenced all around Lexis' team.

Daniel stepped up to the plate, which was a red Frisbee. He prepared to swing. Will sent out the pitch and the outfielders leaned in, prepared to make an out.

Daniel kicked as hard as he could and missed, slipping on the Frisbee and falling down on his behind.

Laughter broke out all around as Ryan helped him to his feet again. He was not deterred. Will sent out the second pitch, and this time Daniel kicked the ball straight in between second and third base.

The ball touched the ground and bounced up into the air. Kaitlin went wild cheering her father's powerful kick as he lunged forward, determined to reach first base.

Greg caught the ball and threw it to Christina, who threw it to Rachel on first. Daniel was running as if his life depended on it, but the sand slowed him down. Just as he reached the plate, Rachel caught the ball and tagged him out.

Again, cheers from Greg's team. Sympathy and support from Daniel's.

I was up. I nodded to Samantha to get ready. Her daddy, Scott, stood by as the pitch came toward me.

The ball sailed toward me. I kicked gently. Fortunately, the ball was made of soft rubber. Even though I was wearing sandals, it didn't hurt my toes. The ball rolled three feet directly in front of me. After punting I yelled to Samantha, "Run for first!"

She took off.

Will ran toward me, picked up the ball and threw it to Rachel, but he overthrew, and Rachel left the base to recover it.

Our team went wild and urged Samantha to keep running. Scott ran along beside her, leading her to second base. Rachel grabbed the ball and threw it to Greg on second, but Samantha ducked under the ball, and reached the base before Greg could make the out.

Our team went wild again and cheered Samantha for her awesome base running. Samantha continued to run, beaming at her success. Her daddy could not have been more proud.

"I knew you could run fast. Now make it home, Samantha!"

She ran as fast as her little legs could carry her and touched home plate, a second before Will tried to tag her out.

People continued to gather up on the boardwalk above, watching the game.

I looked up and noticed that Dr. Griffin, Fancy and her master were gone. What was the connection?

The game ended with a score of nine to five in favor of Will's team. Kevin, who turned out to be in little league, made four of the winning runs alone.

Some of the family stayed behind to enjoy the beach, but Mother and I trekked up the staircase. Even though my brothers carried the chairs for me, my heart began racing from all the energy the stairs took.

Almost there.

We reached the hotel — all tuckered out, ready for a shower to get rid of the sand. Time for my lunch date.

Emily had agreed to meet me for lunch at JRDN, Tower

23's contemporary upscale restaurant only a few blocks away. Being in such a hurry, there was no time to check in with Cecilia.

I rushed downstairs and out through the lobby.

14 Emily Woods

Walking toward the Tower 23 Hotel, I kept an eye out for Fancy.

A dog up ahead...on the right.

Was that her? But as I got closer, I could see it wasn't.

The boardwalk was crowded with tourists. A couple on a tandem bicycle rode by. I stood aside so they could pass. It was tempting to peek into shops along the way, but tee shirts and sundresses really weren't my thing. Besides, Emily was expecting me at noon sharp.

My destination was on the left, a translucent, exquisitely-crafted piece of architecture resembling a glass box, which mirrored the different elements of sun, sea and sky as they changed during the day and into the night.

I had eaten dinner there before. After sunset, the hotel shimmered. There was a dramatic display of contemporary lighting, including a seventy-foot wave wall which changed colors, giving the illusion that you were part of a beautiful painting come to life.

Emily sat in the waiting area. Soft jazz played, which added a touch of elegance. Without any greeting, our host seated us at an inside table with a lovely view of the ocean. Emily's conservative print dress matched her demeanor. She waited for me to speak first.

We casually perused the menus. I told her to order anything she liked. My treat. She was unruffled at the gesture but thanked me. She had chosen JRDN (probably a contemporary spelling of Jordan), the most expensive restaurant on the beach. I remembered the restaurant's description on a flyer in the hotel.

"The look of JRDN is fresh, cool, clean and upbeat. The atmosphere transforms from California casual to West Coast hip as the day advances. Each evening, the dramatic setting sun, for which Pacific Beach is famous, is celebrated by an ambient reflection on a seventy-foot long "wave wall" inside the restaurant. Color-changing lighting continues this theatrical effect throughout the evening."

"Too bad we can't watch the sunset along the wave wall. Have you eaten here before?" I asked.

Emily continued looking at the menu.

"I've been here a few times. The food is organic, that's what I like about it."

The server appeared, dressed in a white shirt and black apron, to take our order.

"What can I get for you to drink?"

"Go ahead, Emily."

"Pellegrino, please."

"And I'll have cranberry juice."

"Would you care for a starter?"

Emily didn't hesitate.

"I'll have the flat bread with the mushroom duxelle, arugula, garlic chips, Parmesan, and truffle oil, please."

"And for you, ma'am?"

"I'll have the artisanal cheese plate, please."

This house specialty sounded lovely — a selection of international creameries served with seasonal fruit accompaniments, honeycomb, and toast. Yummy!

"I'll return with your drinks and take your order."

She left. It was time to begin the questions. I handed Emily my card and she slipped it into her purse.

"That's in case you ever want to talk. Tell me about you and Victoria, you were best friends, I think."

"Yeah, since high school."

Emily looked at me sadly. It was apparent she had taken the loss of her friend hard. Before she could speak, Dr. Griffin came in and walked directly to our table. He was not smiling. If anything, he looked concerned.

"Hello, ladies. Mind if I join you? It looks like you are the two most interesting people in the room. What are you having?"

He sat as the server brought our drinks. She looked as surprised as I did at our new guest. He acted confident.

Emily looked guilty at having lunch with me.

I ordered the meatloaf sandwich and Emily ordered the Tower 23 burger. Dr. Griffin ordered nothing.

Emily shifted in her chair like Dr. Griffin was intimidating her somehow. The air was heavy with tension.

"Dr. Griffin, I'm Jillian Bradley, Chase Campbell's *aunt*." I didn't feel like offering my hand to someone who seemed so hostile.

"Oh, I see now," he said, "and you're interrogating everyone because…."

"Because we believe he's innocent, and because our family only has today before we're scheduled to leave and we'd like for my nephew to leave with us."

Emily looked at me and then turned to him.

"It's okay — I haven't said anything, Dr. Griffin."

"And I don't think you should. This woman has no right to question anyone."

"So you were at the party. You're a very open-minded doctor, they say."

"And who are *they*?" he asked.

I smiled, mirroring his confidence.

"Let's just say it's from a reliable source. There is only one question that needs answering."

He eyed me suspiciously and asked, "What's that?"

I looked directly at Emily. "Who else besides Victoria's boyfriend was at the party?"

She looked as if she was going to tell me but Dr. Griffin took her by the arm and pulled her to her feet.

"That's it, lady. We're leaving now. You should mind your own business and let the police handle this. You'll be better off. Come on, Emily. We need to leave."

The incident was embarrassing to say the least, especially when the server brought two entrees to the table. A few people stared as they left.

Emily looked over her shoulder with pleading in her eyes. We wouldn't be meeting out in the open anymore, but there was always the phone.

With lunch so disrupted, I suddenly lost my appetite and got the order to go. On the walk back to the hotel, the same question kept bothering me.

What was it Emily was trying to hide? Dr. Griffin dealing drugs? A good possibility if Annika saw him give Ecstasy to Victoria.

Was Fancy's owner the supplier? Another good possibility, since Mom saw him with Victoria and I saw him with Dr. Griffin at the kickball game this morning. Emily could be a liability to him if it were true.

What if Dr. Griffin was the murderer? Would he kill Emily to keep her quiet? Was that why they were killed? And if this were all true, what could be done about it? The only person I knew who could help would be Walter — he'd tell me what to do.

Reaching the hotel, I entered through the gate, and looked around to see if there were family members about. Sure enough, most of my family was at the pool. I slid my key through the pool gate and made the rounds.

Paige saw me first.

"Is that a doggie bag, Jillian?"

"Yes, my luncheon didn't exactly work out, so I wound up bringing home both entrees, but don't worry, Teddy will make good use of the hamburger, trust me."

"Who did you have lunch with?"

"Emily Woods and Dr. Reed Griffin, friends of the victims, who are hiding something about what happened by the way they acted."

"Wow, hope you get somewhere soon — Brooke and Greg are getting discouraged with nothing happening. Have you talked to everyone?"

"I've talked to the twins and Mom. I've also talked to Will, but not about the murders."

"Have you heard the latest?"

"Not since last night."

"Will went over to see Stephanie just about an hour ago. Something must be going on with those two."

"It's obvious that Will still loves her — question is, does she still love him?"

"That's what I think. Sure hope he doesn't get hurt again. Lexis and Annika don't know what to think. I've talked to them about it, and they both aren't very happy about her showing up like this. Do you think she's after his money?"

"Not really, but it's possible. She seems gainfully employed and independent. It's interesting, though, that she's never remarried. It might mean she still loves him."

My phone rang. It was an unidentified caller. "Excuse me a minute, Paige."

She nodded to go ahead.

"Hello?"

"Can you talk where no one can hear you? It's Emily."

My heart skipped a beat.

"I'm leaving the pool right now. Go ahead."

"Just make sure there's no one around before you answer me. I'll wait."

"Okay." I remained silent until I got to my room, opened the door, and sat in the chair. "Go ahead, Emily. I'm listening."

"You wanted to know who else was at the party. I'll tell you. It was a man named Alex Draper. He's a friend of Dr.

Griffin."

"And a friend of Victoria's?"

Emily was silent for a moment.

"He was more of an acquaintance. She never hung out with him, really. He just liked being around all her rich friends."

"Did you tell the police he was there?"

"No."

"You figured you would redirect their attention, is that it?"

"I'm really sorry, Jillian. What else was there to think! He was there when she was killed."

"But so were you, Emily."

"I know, I know. But I had no reason to kill her."

"And you think Chase did? Why, because of the argument they had in the hot tub? What really happened that night, anyway?"

"Look, Victoria got a little moody when she was drunk, and when Chase tried taking her drink away...."

"Why did he do that?"

"She was starting to use bad language and there were kids around. It looked like Chase was trying to help her."

"If you think that, why didn't you tell the police the truth instead of letting them think he was getting too personal?"

"Because at first I really thought he killed her. He was the last person to see her alive besides me, so that's why I said what I did."

"Okay, it's going to be hard to change your story. But, Emily — you can't let Chase pay for something he didn't do."

"You're right, but you don't understand."

I didn't speak for a moment, waiting for her to tell me what was bothering her. But she was silent.

"Emily, I do understand that Dr. Griffin doesn't want you talking to me for some reason. Could you get someone in trouble, possibly, if you do?"

"Yes, but that's all I can tell you. I have to go. Please don't try and call me."

"If that's what you want, but think about what I've said."

The call ended without her even saying goodbye, as if someone had just come in and interrupted her.

I had almost forgotten Cecilia had Teddy.

When I reached her room she greeted me warmly. Teddy ran to greet me and wagged his tail with vigor, begging me to pick him up.

"How was lunch?" she asked.

Teddy almost leaped into my arms, he was so glad to see me. Hugs followed and a kiss. He licked my hand, but not for affection (it was the salt on my skin that attracted him), but it felt like affection, so I chose to take it that way.

"All I can say is my poking around is upsetting Dr. Griffin. He showed up right after we ordered and took Emily away, almost by force."

"How strange."

"She just called me. At least I had presence of mind enough to give her one of my cards before he showed up."

"Did you learn anything?"

"Something very important. The name of the other man who was at the party was Alex Draper, a drug dealer perhaps. Anyway, it should be interesting to see how he ties into this whole thing."

"Cecilia, please get all you can on Dr. Griffin. Find out where he works, who his patients are, where he trained, what clubs he belongs to, everything you can."

"I'm on it. Just give me a minute to save my article. Would you like me to check on Alex Draper, too?"

"Please. I'm going to meet Lee for tea in a little while. I'll see what I can find out from him."

"You're meeting Lee Sterling? Careful, Jillian. You know the kind of men you're attracted to."

"Whatever do you mean, my dear?"

"Are you serious? Jillian, remember Vincent Fontaine in Scottsdale, how you got tied up with him?"

"That was different. That was business-related, Cecilia."

"Right. And what about Ira Sinclair? Need I go on?"

For a fleeting moment, fond thoughts about those men crossed my mind, but then I suppressed them and focused on what needed to be done at the present — getting Chase out of jail!

I sighed grimly and hugged Teddy all the more.

"Everything's okay, He just needs someone to talk to right now. You wouldn't understand. I hope you never have to."

She walked over to me and put her hand on my shoulder.

"I'm sorry. I'm only thinking of you."

"I know. Call me if you find anything on Dr. Griffin. It's time for me to meet Lee."

"Where are you going?"

"The Mad Dog Café."

15 Lee Sterling

Lee was waiting for me at a small white table on the patio of The Mad Dog Café. He halfway smiled when he saw me turn the corner and walk toward him.

There were only a few people having afternoon tea. For fun, we ordered crumpets, the café's signature offering. He suggested we eat on the patio where we could be alone. That was fine with me.

We found a table, then Lee took the tea and crumpets off the tray. He pulled out my chair for me.

"Thank you." He had such good manners. "And thank you for meeting me."

I sipped my hot tea and took a dainty bite of crumpet.

"Believe me," he said, "the pleasure is all mine. Sometimes it gets overwhelming with everything on my plate. I needed to get away from it all."

"Understandable. How is Victoria's producer taking all of this?"

"It's sick. They all look at it as promotional." He took a sip of tea and a bite of crumpet covered in butter and honey.

I sat my tea down.

"Well, that's how they are in show business. Lee, I tried to have lunch today with Emily."

"I know. Reed told me all about it."

"He did? What's his problem? He was really rude."

"He means well, just looking out for me, I guess. It's bad enough with the media wanting stories. Don't worry too much about him."

"If you say so. Have you talked to any reporters yet?"

"No. And I don't intend to. There are at least twenty calls on my voicemail. Jillian, I don't want to have anything to do with any of it. Why can't they leave me alone and let me get on with my business?"

Taking a bite of my crumpet, I said nothing. There's a trick to getting information from someone — just wait. The other person will usually say something of interest, at least most of the time.

Lee set his tea down and looked at the table.

"Sometimes I wonder if it was worth it. All the hard work I do, all the travel, all the difficult clients I have to deal with. I don't know. Used to think I was doing it for Birdie and Victoria, but after they were successful on their own, it didn't feel like they really needed me."

"Did you ever talk to Birdie about how you felt?"

"No. She never had the time, and we hardly talked anymore. You might say we went in different directions. But I honestly loved them. Really loved them! And now, it's too late." He buried his face in his hands.

"I'm so sorry, Lee. I know it hurts. But my sister and brother-in-law will also be hurt if their son is convicted of murder. He didn't kill your wife or Victoria, I'd bet my life on it."

Lee shrugged his shoulders and looked at his empty cup.

"That's a big bet. Look, I don't know what you're looking for, but I can't think of anything that will help you."

"Maybe not. What about Dr. Griffin? Would he have any motive?"

Lee shifted in his chair.

"What do you mean?"

"Well, I happen to know that someone saw him give

Victoria Ecstasy, and if he thought he could lose his medical practice, that would certainly be a motive."

"It's time we ended this conversation, Jillian. Reed may or may not have done what you said, but you have to understand that you're getting a little too personal now."

This was the second time today someone embarrassed me and it was starting to make me angry. Even so, his comment hurt, and the color rose to my face. Regaining my composure was difficult. Why did he have to be so attractive, anyway?

"I'm sorry, Lee." Refocus. He did not respond to my apology — the silence made me feel extremely uncomfortable.

Why was he so protective of Dr. Griffin?

"I'm just looking at all the angles here. But I do understand," I finally said. The conversation was over. I pushed back my chair and stood.

He did the same.

"Thanks again for the tea." I turned and started to leave. Again, there was no response. I glanced at him one last time to see what he would do, but he turned and walked away.

It was truly puzzling! How could he have turned on my friendship so suddenly? Unless he felt true allegiance to Dr. Griffin. Was that what it was? Allegiance? I wasn't convinced.

Foot traffic grew heavier as I walked slowly to the hotel, trying to shake off the slight. More tourists. More couples passing by....

"It's okay," I muttered, "Whatever it takes to find out the truth for Chase's sake, I'll do. Just remember that, Jillian!"

After the pep talk, I thought about what Lee had said, that Dr. Griffin "looked out for him." What could that mean? I hoped Cecilia had found out something by the time I returned.

Looking at the different people passing, I wondered if

any of them had secrets. Secret lovers? Secret cheating on test scores for college? Lying to the IRS? What kind of secrets do people have?

There were a few homeless people about, either lying on a bench asleep or walking with backpacks holding all their worldly possessions. Did any of them have secrets?

Deflated, I finally reached the lobby and took the elevator to my floor. Now Lee was alienated, but maybe it was for the best.

Cecilia and Teddy greeted me after I knocked on her door.

"How did your date go?"

"Terrible. I'll probably never see him again."

Cecilia looked surprised.

"What on earth happened?"

"I was just honest and told him about Dr. Griffin giving Ecstasy to Victoria at the party. It really upset him! He's defensive of Griffin for some reason."

I took off my shoes and sat in the chair, feeling depressed. Teddy jumped into my lap. Just holding the little fella made me feel better.

"Well," she said, "I've done some digging, and I think you might be right. Dr. Griffin has an interesting record of client complaints about his lack of professionalism in dealing with them."

"Anything illegal, though?"

"There are a couple of questionable lawsuits he's been in. It seems he also provided a false testimony on one occasion."

"That sounds interesting. Anything else?"

"You asked about his patients. It turns out that the only patients he had were the Sterlings."

"So am I to understand that he lost his practice due to the false testimony?"

"Sure sounds like it. Wonder why the Sterlings used him?"

"Isn't it obvious? Must have something to do with Victoria. Cecilia, I need to talk to Emily again. She's gone home and I don't know how to get in touch with her."

"Let me see about getting the information for you. It might be difficult."

"Wait a minute. I have an idea. The hotel would have her information, wouldn't they?"

"Probably. What are you thinking?"

"Well, if I could use their computer…."

"No, Jillian. You can't do any hacking!"

"You're right. Maybe it won't be necessary. There's someone who might tell me where she lives."

"Who do you know in San Diego?"

"Someone who knew Victoria. That pizza delivery guy. He must live around here." My instincts told me he just might cooperate. "I bet I can track him down through his work. If I could talk to him, he might tell me where Emily lives."

"How are you going to do that?"

"I remember Emily saying they all went to the same high school. It's worth a try, anyway. What else are we going to do?"

"You're right. It's worth a shot."

"I'm going down to the lobby and talk to the concierge. They'll know where the pizza place is. Let me grab a cab and see if I can track him down. His name is Josh, I think, and I can give a good description.

"Cecilia, you hold down the fort with Teddy here." I handed him to her. He looked at me with pleading eyes as if asking, "Why can't I go with you?"

"I'm sorry, baby, but you can't go into the pizza place." Teddy whimpered as if he understood. What an amazing dog he was! I really hated to leave him.

"I'll return as soon as I can."

"Jillian, please be careful. Call me when you've found out anything and let me know you're okay."

"Don't worry. I will." I kissed Teddy on top of his head. "We'll practice our commands together when I get home, okay?"

The concierge told me the name of the pizza place — Liberty Pizza, between Feldspar and Mission. The address was within walking distance, but I opted to have her call a cab for me. I might need one to go see Emily, if I could find her. I must find her.

I knew what I needed to do. Pray.

"Lord God, I need You right now. Please help me locate this girl so I can find out the truth. Amen."

The cab arrived and asked for the address. He nodded and we drove away. It only took a few minutes before we pulled up and parked in front of the place. The sign on the front had the statue of liberty holding a pizza. Okay, I got it. New York style pizza. Whatever!

"Please wait here," I said. It didn't matter if the meter was ticking.

"Sure, ma'am," said the driver.

I walked up to the counter searching the kitchen to see if Josh was working. He wasn't around anywhere. "Is Josh working tonight?" I asked casually. The young girl at the counter nodded.

"Yeah, he's out on a delivery. He left a while ago so he should be here any second. Can I get you some pizza?"

"No thank you, I'll just sit and wait for him." I stepped aside for the next person in line.

I waited for three long minutes jiggling my leg up and down until the back door finally opened and Josh came in. The girl at the counter spoke to him and gestured toward me.

He came over to where I sat.

"Hi. You wanted to see me?" He looked only slightly nervous.

"Yes, it will only take a minute. You see, I'm trying to get in touch with Emily Woods. She, ah, has something for me. Thought you might know where she lives. She said you went to high school with her."

Josh relaxed a little, which was a good sign.

He nodded. "I have all that stuff at home. Just finished my last delivery. Did the afternoon shift today. You want to come with me? I'll get it for you, if you like."

"Thanks, I really appreciate it. Do you need a lift? I have a cab outside."

"That'd be great. Otherwise, I'd have to walk. I don't live too far."

We both got in the car, and Josh gave the driver his address. Josh seemed a bit nervous, but he thanked me again for the ride after we got inside.

"How did you meet Emily?" he asked.

I didn't want to seem like a nosy old woman so I thought of a way to phrase my answer so it wouldn't be a lie.

"We met at the hotel...after the tragedy. She and Victoria were very close, weren't they?"

"Best friends." He tapped the driver on the shoulder, and pointed. "This is it."

We stopped in front of a small beach cottage, and I again asked the driver to wait.

Josh unlocked the front door and motioned for me to step inside. The house was quiet except for a parakeet fluttering in its cage over in a corner.

"That's Peety. Had him for two years now. He keeps me company when Grandma's at work."

"So you live here with her?"

"Yeah, I kind of look out after her. Have a seat. I'll go get my directory. Our school put it out so the parents could keep up with us. Like that would happen, right?"

"Couldn't say. I don't have any children."

He nodded and went down the hall. There was a newspaper on the coffee table, so I picked it up. The headline read, Murderer Suspect Caught. Thinking about Chase, a twinge of nausea washed over me.

Josh returned with the directory in his hand.

"Here it is. I found Emily's address for you." He pointed to the back of the directory under 'W' and handed it to me.

"Great. Let me write that down. I have a pen here and a card to write on."

As I was writing the address, I handed him one of my cards. "If you ever want to talk about Victoria, please give me a call."

He took it and seemed impressed that I was a gardening columnist for three papers.

"I can show you where she lives, if you want," he said.

"Thanks, I appreciate that, but I think I can manage with the cab."

"Whatever." He shrugged.

"Thanks for finding the address for me. I need to be going."

He closed the door rather slowly after I left, and I wondered if he had any friends. He seemed lonely. My motherly instincts were getting the better of me. Focus on Emily! She must have answers — she was right there when Victoria was murdered!

The cab driver smiled at me, no doubt thinking about the fare he would collect.

"Where to next?" he asked.

I handed him the address and we were off.

Emily's house was in a modest neighborhood where all the houses had neatly trimmed yards and picket fences. Colorful flowers bloomed in boxes suspended from the porch ceiling. I approached the front door and knocked. There was no answer. I knocked again and turned to look at the cab driver, confirming I wanted him to wait. The door opened a crack. Emily peered out.

"What do you want, Jillian?"

"We need to talk, Emily. May I please come in?"

"You can if you get rid of that cab. Nothing like being obvious!"

I paid the driver and thanked him for being so patient. He drove off. Maybe it was a mistake coming here alone.

Emily opened the door and ushered me inside. She wouldn't look me in the eye.

"There's no one here right now, otherwise, I would have acted like I didn't know you. Why are you trying to get me in trouble?"

"I'm not trying to get you in trouble. I just need to talk to you because whether you know it or not, you may help me see things more clearly. Do you have a problem with that?"

"Okay, fine! But if my parents come home, you're a salesman or taking a survey, okay?"

"Agreed."

She didn't ask me to sit down.

"What do you want to ask me?"

"For starters, what happened to Dr. Griffin's practice?"

She looked surprised by the question.

"Don't know what to tell you. He's been her doctor for as long as I've known her. He's a family friend."

"Yes, I got that. But why is he so defensive in all this? I mean, sure he's just lost two thirds of his practice, and I'd be upset too, believe me, but why is he so devoted to the Sterlings?"

Emily remained standing and crossed her arms.

"I can see you're not going to give up until you find out, so I might as well tell you. Besides, it's my fault that it even happened."

"What happened, Emily?"

"Victoria had an abortion, and Dr. Griffin performed it for her."

"Why do you think that was your fault?"

"Because Victoria told her mom she was spending the night with me the night it happened. She went to a party instead. She told me she got pretty wasted. Then some guy gave her a date rape drug, and she was raped repeatedly.

She doesn't remember what happened, but the next morning she felt horrible.

"Victoria didn't deserve what happened to her. She was just in the wrong place with the wrong people. Anyway, she called me the next morning to come get her and made me promise never to tell anyone. She was so ashamed. And I never did...until just now."

This new information made me think differently of Victoria. Perhaps she was standoffish and depressed because of the attack. Just because a girl sneaked out like that didn't mean she deserved such violence.

And then, of course, her status as a public figure would pressure her to...I suddenly felt sad about the loss of an innocent life. If only she had confided in someone, someone who really cared for her. Someone she trusted.

"So Dr. Griffin was kept on by Victoria because he did the abortion?"

"That was part of the reason. He also promised never to tell anyone."

"And the other part?" Emily uncrossed her arms and began pacing nervously.

"Victoria used cocaine, but only occasionally."

I tried not to look shocked, but I knew I didn't succeed.

"You're surprised, aren't you? But a lot of people use it to stay awake so they can work longer. That's why Victoria did. Sometimes her schedule at the studio was so grueling she felt like she had no other choice to keep going."

"I suppose that's typical with many users. Come to think of it, I've even known people who used it for the same reason."

"Anyway, we went together to Dr. Griffin's office to get the abortion. I was against her not telling her mom, but Victoria said it would destroy her. She told me she would get one with or without me, so that's why I went with her.

"She told Birdie we were going to the mall. When we got home, Victoria looked really bad, but she told Birdie it was that time of the month and that she would be fine. Birdie never knew.

"Jillian, if I hadn't lied for her that night, she wouldn't have gone to the party!"

Emily pressed her hands to her temples, as if to keep herself from totally breaking down. She had harbored an awful guilt that was painfully real.

"Emily, you don't know that. She would have gone to one eventually — don't you see? It wasn't your fault. People make their own choices in this life. Victoria was a victim of a cruel crime, but you are not responsible for that. Place the blame where the blame is due."

"Well, now you know. Dr. Griffin is just trying to protect her memory."

"Maybe. But I wonder what else he's hiding. Did you ever hear him say anything about a former patient that sounded out of the ordinary?"

Emily stopped and furrowed her brow. "I can't think of anything."

I took a card out of my purse and handed it to her.

"If you think of anything more, please call me. It may be important."

"Okay, if it doesn't get me in trouble."

"So you think Dr. Griffin would harm you? Why? Has he harmed anyone before?"

Emily looked nervous. "I think you'd better leave."

"If that's what you want," I said, "I'll call a cab."

"Please have them pick you up at the corner. I'm sorry, but I don't want anyone to know you've been here."

This girl really was scared.

"Fine. I'll do what you ask. I hope you don't come to any harm. If you think you're in danger, you should really call the police, Emily."

She just looked away and shut the door behind me.

I walked down the street to wait at the corner for the cab.

16 Alex Draper and Fancy

By the time I got back to the hotel, I felt depressed. To me, Emily didn't seem like the type to get plastered and pass out at a party. But how else was she so knocked out that she didn't hear the intruder that night?

Chase? Yes, I could see him drinking that much, being the age he was and a guy, but it didn't make sense that Emily would. What if someone put something in her drink and knocked her out? If it happened to Victoria, it could have happened to Emily, which would mean that someone at the party doctored her drink.

Would Dr. Griffin do such a thing? Perhaps. If Tucker Shaw doctored her drink and Victoria ever found out, it would jeopardize their relationship, so it didn't make sense to suspect him. That left only one other person. Alex Draper.

Now, how to find him?

Cecilia!

"There you are!" she said as she answered the door. "Come on in."

Teddy popped his little head up from his towel. Perhaps some love from him was just what I needed. I picked him up and held him close.

"Yes, I know I promised to play with you and we'll practice our commands soon, but for now you get to play in Brooke's room. Cecilia, any news from Walter?"

"He's busy working on a new case. Hasn't found out anything on Dr. Griffin, but he said sometimes you have to study things from different angles."

When she said that, something clicked in my brain.

"Cecilia, you've given me an idea."

"I have?"

She looked pleased.

"What if there's something in Dr. Griffin's past that doesn't show up. How would he hide it?"

She furrowed her brow.

"I really don't know since I've never tried to hide anything. I'll ask Walter. If anyone knows, he will. Here, I'll send him a quick e-mail." She went to the computer and her fingers flew across the keyboard.

"Good." I started pacing a little, unable to sit still. "Emily told me that Dr. Griffin gave Victoria an abortion."

"Wow! That's big news! And you think he held it over her head?"

"Maybe. It sounds like something underhanded might be going on, at any rate."

"Hmm. Have you had dinner? I'm starving! I've fed Teddy for you."

"Thanks. I'm getting hungry, too. What sounds good?"

"I'd kind of like to go out. I've been in the room all day."

"Then let's do that. I'll get Brooke to watch Teddy. She's offered many times. And I'll ask her to have the kids practice his commands."

Cecilia was dressed and ready to go — she held Teddy for me while I went to my room, touched up my hair and lipstick and grabbed a light jacket. The nights here got chilly next to the ocean.

We checked in with Brooke. She took Teddy from me, hugging him gently.

"He'll keep the kids entertained. They can't wait to play with him."

I knew it would get Brooke's mind off Chase for a while. The police had placed him in a holding cell in the county jail where he had been booked. He was now waiting for arraignment. At least he had a lawyer.

I gave Brooke a hug of encouragement and Teddy a quick kiss goodbye.

As we walked out from Brooke's patio to go to the boardwalk, I noticed Lee sitting at a table having a drink with Dr. Griffin. I nodded politely, but neither of them acknowledged.

So it was going to be like that.

Oh, well, what goes around comes around. If either of them were hiding anything I would find out what it was.

The air was on the chilly side, but it was still a lovely evening. We watched a soft breeze waft through the palm trees and heard the ocean's gentle roar.

Cecilia inhaled deeply. She looked happy to be outdoors.

"Where are we going?" she asked.

"No place in particular. We'll see what looks interesting."

I stopped suddenly and touched Cecilia's arm.

"Jillian, what is it?"

"Over there, that man and his dog, the apricot poodle."

"I see them. What about them?"

"I've met them once before, taking Teddy for a walk. That man was talking to Dr. Griffin when we were playing kickball this morning. Come on."

We walked over to where the two sat on a patch of grass. The man looked up and smiled, seeming happy to see me again.

"Hello, there," he said. "Where's Teddy tonight?"

"My assistant and I are going out for dinner, so I left him with my sister. Cecilia, this is...I'm sorry, I don't know your name."

He stood and offered his hand. "I'm Alex Draper, and this is Fancy, my best friend."

Cecilia shook his hand and offered it for Fancy to smell. "It's nice to meet you."

Fancy approved and allowed Cecilia to pet her.

"And I'm Jillian."

We shook hands.

"Where are you going for dinner?" he asked.

"We don't know yet," I said, "wherever strikes our fancy. No pun intended!"

Fancy whimpered.

Alex patted her head. "She's such a big baby. Even scared of her own name."

"And yet you sometimes leave her tied up." Why did I say that?

He looked at me with sudden alertness.

"Yeah, sometimes. But I've trained her to attack anyone who messes with her while I'm gone, so there's really no need to worry about her when I do. You didn't try to pet her, did you?"

"No, at first she snarled at us, but after she sensed we weren't going to hurt her, she just acted scared. Why would you leave her alone like that?"

He cocked his head.

"Hey, you look familiar. Are you some kind of celebrity? I know I've seen your picture somewhere before."

"Maybe you have." I took out a card and handed it to him. "Here's my card. Perhaps you've seen the *Ask Jillian* column in *The San Francisco Enterprise*. Have you ever read my column?"

"Yeah, once or twice. Sometimes I find newspapers floating around here after people have used them for blankets, if you know what I mean."

Cecilia started to look ill. "I'm sorry but I think we'd better eat. I'm feeling a little nauseous."

"We have to go. It was nice to meet you finally. Take care."

"Let's eat at the first place we see," I said.

The Tower 23 Hotel loomed ahead on the left. "Let's eat here, at JRDN. It doesn't look too crowded."

The sun hadn't really started to set yet so I told the host to seat us anywhere. We ordered and Cecilia began to nibble on the bread and butter.

"I see your appetite has returned," I said.

"Would you mind if I ordered a steak?"

"Whatever you like. On me, of course."

"Of course." She smiled. "I really appreciate it, Jillian."

"Well, I appreciate your coming with me. Besides, who else am I going to spend my money on?"

"What about your family? Your nieces and nephews?"

"Their families are all well off. No, other than spending money on my art collection, I suppose I like giving to the Humane Society and the Red Cross. I feel so sorry for those poor homeless animals and for people who go through disasters. Of course, it's also a blessing for me to give to my church. I mean, if people didn't give, they'd become selfish, don't you think?"

"I wouldn't know. Giving is something I need to work on. Hold on, I have an e-mail coming in, it may be from Walter." She read the message and closed her phone.

"Walter says sometimes people expunge records so they won't show up in credit reports or in job applications. He says if someone is taken to trial and found not guilty, the charge can be hidden as if it never happened."

"I see. Interesting. That means the good doctor may have done something illegal. Maybe even gone to trial, but got off somehow. Hmm. That *is* interesting."

"But even if that's true, how would you ever find out anything?"

"The same way I find out everything else. I ask questions."

"Do you think Dr. Griffin would talk to you?"

"He might not, but maybe someone else will. I'm so sorry to have to leave you this way but I really need to go and find Alex Draper. I must talk to him. Why don't you stay here and eat your dinner…."

"What if he's not there?"

"If he's not there, save my dinner and I'll be back."

"Okay, Jillian. No problem. I've known you long enough to understand how your mind works! Good luck, and *please* be careful."

The server brought our food and set it down, just as I got up. I put on my jacket and headed out the door.

"Lord," I prayed, "please help me find Alex. I must talk to him. He may be the only link to get Chase freed. Amen."

Walking to where I saw them before, I started searching the crowd. They were not where I left them. I looked toward the hotel and made out a man walking with a dog. Stepping up my pace, almost breaking into a run, I caught up behind them. Alex turned around when he heard me approach.

"Hey! Did you forget something?" he asked.

"Yes, as a matter of fact. I was wondering if I could talk to you about Victoria."

Alex looked around, probably looking for Cecilia.

"Looks like you're all alone. Where's your friend?" he said mockingly.

A slight wariness crept over me.

"She'll be here in a minute," I said, hoping I was right. "Are you going to answer my question?"

I didn't back down.

"Look, I really can't talk here."

"Then call me. If you don't, my nephew's blood may be on your hands. I'll be waiting, Alex. Goodbye, Fancy."

Alex stood there looking undecided.

I couldn't tell if he was just nice on the outside and evil on the inside, but hopefully, he would come through with something that would help Chase. I smiled a little, turned and walked to find Cecilia.

She met me coming out the door, holding my entrée in a

doggie bag.

"Did you find him? What happened?"

"With God's help, I found him. He wouldn't say anything when I asked him about Victoria, but I told him to call me or Chase's blood may be on his hands."

"You are something else, Jillian. What if he killed them? What if he tries to kill *you* for poking around asking questions? Have you thought about that?"

"No, it doesn't matter what happens to me. Chase is the important one here, don't you see? The police are probably doing everything they can to prove Chase is guilty — we're the only ones who are trying to prove he's innocent. You know that."

"You're right. But you have to stop taking chances like that."

We were almost to the hotel when my phone rang. The caller's number was unfamiliar.

"Jillian?"

Emily.

"Yes, Emily? Are you okay?"

"I'm fine. I just remembered something and thought it might be helpful."

"That's good, go ahead."

"After Chase and Tucker broke the table top, two guys came in and replaced it with a new one."

"That's correct."

"Well, while one of them was cleaning up the glass, the other one went over to the bar and was supposedly clearing away some empty bottles. I was watching him."

"What did he do?"

"I'm not exactly sure, but I caught him looking at me. It was only for a second and I looked away. There was just this feeling he was doing something he wasn't supposed to be doing. I know it's not much, but I thought I'd tell you."

"Thanks, it may be something. Emily, I hate to ask, but are you a heavy sleeper, or were you out that night because of alcohol?"

"Let's just say I'm not a heavy sleeper."

"Got it. Getting back to what you just told me, I haven't checked out all the staff who were there yet, but I will for sure now. Would you recognize him if you saw him again?"

"I've got to go," she said nervously and hung up.

Rats!

"Cecilia, I've missed one other person who was there that night, and he could be the killer. Emily hung up before she said she'd be willing to identify him."

"You don't think Alex could have killed them?"

"Granted, I've seen Alex with Dr. Griffin after the murders, and granted, Emily has identified him as being at the party. But my heart says he didn't kill them."

"Your heart? Well, you might be right. What we don't have is proof."

"Or motive."

"But if Dr. Griffin thought Victoria was going to reveal he did the abortion, wouldn't that backfire on her career?"

"Maybe. Or maybe the abortion had nothing to do with it."

"You think it was something else? Like what?"

"Like whatever Dr. Griffin is hiding. I need to talk to Miguel again and see who else was working that night. Someone helped Lucas with that tabletop."

Cecilia took Teddy to her room (along with my doggie bag), and I went to the lobby looking for Miguel.

"Good evening, Mrs. Bradley," said the concierge who worked the desk. "How can I help you this evening?"

There had been bad vibes coming from this woman ever since I had asked her who Dr. Griffin was.

"Good evening. I'm looking for Miguel Ramirez. Is he working tonight by any chance?"

She hesitated.

"Can I help you with anything?"

"I just need to talk to Miguel if he's here."

"Let me check and see if he's on the schedule. One moment, please." She typed something into the computer and scanned it briefly. "He is working somewhere on the property, I'm not sure where. Would you like for me to leave him a message that you want to talk to him?"

"That would be appreciated. Thanks." I started to leave, but hesitated.

"Just one more thing, if you don't mind. Your night auditor, does he work on the weekends or just week nights?"

She was really sending out negative vibes now, but I chose not to notice.

"Our night auditor only works week nights," she said coldly. "We use a service on the weekend. Is there anything else?"

"No, that's all. I'll see if I can find Miguel."

The phone rang and she answered it, turning on the charm once again now that I was leaving.

No one was in the various offices when I peered in. I checked outside and all around the first floor to see if I could locate him.

Maybe Miguel was down in the garage somewhere.

I took the elevator to the ground floor.

The garage was dark and almost empty. Guests had taken their cars and gone out for dinner.

I thought of my family and wished I was having dinner with them, sitting around talking and laughing like we usually did. Now the laughter was gone, replaced by fear and concern for poor Chase.

The Cayman Room was empty, too. I checked the other side of the garage to see if anyone was around. There were sounds of voices and hammering coming from the laundry room. Someone was in there. I walked over to see who it was and found Lucas and Zach working on something in the boiler room.

"Good evening, ma'am," said Lucas. "Can we help

you?"

"Good evening. Just looking for Miguel. Have you seen him anywhere?"

The two men looked at each other and shrugged.

"Haven't seen him for a while," said Lucas. "What do you need?"

"Oh, nothing really. Just wanted to ask him a question about a plant. I write a gardening column and he's helped me before. Have a good evening."

I could feel their eyes boring into my back as I walked away.

Heading up in the elevator to the second floor, I continued to search for Miguel. The halls were empty except for two bikini-clad teenagers on their way to the pool.

As I rounded the corner to check out the last hallway, I almost ran into Connie coming down the stairs. The stairs! A possibility formed in my mind. She saw me and looked a little startled.

"Hello, Mrs. Bradley," she said. "Are you looking for someone?"

"Yes, as a matter of fact. Have you seen Miguel tonight? I really need to talk to him."

"I've seen him around. Is there something I can help you with?"

"I wanted to ask him who the night auditor was on Sunday evening. Do you happen to know?"

She reflected a moment, trying to think.

"It was the guy who works on the weekends. Danny Pratt. Yeah, that's his name."

"Was Danny the one who helped Lucas with the table top? Can you remember?"

"Ah, no. It wasn't Danny. Mrs. Bradley, I need to take care of a guest. Would you please excuse me?"

"Of course. Thanks, Connie."

She scurried off to a room down the hall.

Why didn't she tell me who it was? Was she scared? It sure seemed that way.

I checked out the staircase and walked up to the third floor. The stairs were narrow and concealed, making a perfect escape route for someone who didn't want to be seen.

Did the killer leave this way?

I wondered if he didn't come in this way, too.

Why did I think I could solve this mystery? Doubt crept in that I would ever find the killer. But thinking negatively wasn't going to get me anywhere. *Jillian, force your mind to refocus!* I had one thing the killer didn't. Sheer determination to clear Chase.

I will find you.

17 The Pizza Guy

There was a dogged determination about me now. The pieces of the puzzle were going to come together eventually. There were motives, although none of them were entirely clear. As for opportunity — a number of people could have killed that evening. And means? Someone strong enough and knowledgeable enough to kill with their bare hands.

I walked slowly to my room...Lee? Dr. Griffin? Alex? The phantom worker that night? It didn't matter. Somehow, I would succeed in finding out the truth. After all, God knew *who* the killer was and where he was. Since I knew God, all I had to do was keep asking Him to show me the way. I looked heavenward and prayed silently for help.

Dinner finally sounded good as I knocked on Cecilia's door.

"Hey there," she said. "Bet you're hungry. Want me to heat up your dinner?"

"Yes, thanks. Come here sweet pooch!"

Teddy wagged his tail and flexed his ears in sheer joy. I picked him up and smothered him with lots of love.

"Don't worry, he's had some of my dinner," she said, heating my entrée in the microwave. After a minute, the bell dinged. She carefully took the hot plate, put it on a pot holder and handed it to me.

"You must be exhausted, Jillian."

"This food should help. Thanks. I ran into Connie on the second floor just now, and she gave me the name of the night auditor, a Danny Pratt. We can check him out."

"That's good. Anything else?"

"Yes and no. There was one other person who helped Lucas with the tabletop. I don't know his name yet, but Miguel may know who he was."

After only a few bites, my supper was gone. "Boy, JRDN sure serves small portions, don't they?"

"Yeah," she said. "Guess you could count one of their servings as a half of everyone else's."

"And twice the money. But anyway, it's organic, as Emily pointed out, so it's probably better for you."

I took the plate to the sink and rinsed it off, happy that the housekeepers would do the dishes and not me.

I love vacations. Not having to make my bed, not having to do laundry, no dishes to wash, no cooking, having lovely weather here in San Diego, and the sound of the ocean nearby. I could live here! But alas, it was time to leave tomorrow and still no word from the police about finding the real killer.

"Cecilia, I've decided to stay until the killer is found."

"But that will cost you a fortune! How long?"

"I really don't know. But I'm not leaving tomorrow with the rest of the family. You can go home if you need to and take Teddy with you."

"That's okay. Walter will be fine. He's so into his work I hardly see him anyway. Besides, we stay in touch by phone and e-mail."

My phone rang and gave me a jolt.

"Hello?"

"It's me, Josh, you know, the pizza guy?" He sounded uncertain that I would even remember him. He might not get much attention from anyone.

"Hi, Josh. It's nice to hear from you. What's going on?"

"I, ah, I…I just wondered if you found Emily's house

okay after you left."

"Yes, thanks to you. You know, you were a Godsend."

There was a hesitation before he spoke.

"Yeah?" he said finally. "Good, I'm glad. Hey, thought you might want to know that the police were just here asking a bunch of questions."

"Really? What did they want to know? That is, if you don't mind my asking."

"No, that's okay. I figured they'd come talk to me eventually since I was at the party. They asked me who else was there, did I notice anything unusual, that kind of stuff."

"I'm sure you have a good eye. What did you think of the people who were there? At the party, I mean. Did you know any of them?"

"The only people I knew were Victoria and Emily. And that one guy, Alex Draper. He's bad news, Mrs. Bradley. Sells drugs. I've seen him around."

"Have you actually seen him selling drugs?"

"Well, yeah. I wouldn't say he sold them unless I saw him do it. I delivered a pizza once to a house where I actually saw him."

"That's incredible! What did you see him do?"

"He was in this guy's kitchen. See, the door was open just far enough where I could see in when the guy went to get the money to pay for the pizza. Alex handed this other dude a small package, and the dude gave him cash, real sneaky like. There were drugs all over the place, mostly marijuana by the smell of it."

"What did you do?"

"Are you kidding me? Nothing! I didn't want to get mixed up with any of those people. My grandma has a hard enough time just keeping me in school. I don't need to get into any more trouble. She's been too good to me."

"So, how did you find out that his name was Alex Draper?"

"Well, that's what I wanted to tell you. At Victoria's

party, I see him, right? And he looks at me like he recognizes me, so he comes over and introduces himself as Alex Draper. He asks me if we've met and of course, I say no, which is true, sort of. He's okay with it, but I can tell he's trying to think where he saw me before."

"Did you talk to him after that?"

"No. But he'll figure it out. I delivered the pizza to the party that night."

"Hmm, well, he may. Josh, you know someone broke the tabletop at the party. Did you happen to see who brought up the new one? It might be important."

"Let's see. It was two guys who work at the hotel. They had on hotel uniforms. It might be hard to recognize them, but I might. I'm pretty good at faces."

"I'm sure you are."

"You should see my computer sometime. I could show you all the stuff I have on Victoria."

"Oh my, what kind of stuff?"

"Oh, it's not what you think. There are no nude pictures or anything like that. You know, just stuff about Victoria, like how she started out, different episodes of *It's My Life* that she did. I have nearly all of the information on her that's out there — 50,000 hits so far."

"That sounds like a lot of hits, Josh. That's really amazing! Tell me something. What information do you have that you think no one else has out there? I'd be interested to know."

I could almost hear him thinking over the phone.

"Let me see. Did you know that her little fingers curled in?"

"No. They did?"

"Yeah. And she wasn't as stuck up as some people thought she was."

"You have that on your site?"

"No, I just thought it. I only talked to her once. It was at a football game, and I said, 'Excuse me' when I had to cross in front of her to find a seat. She smiled at me and that's when I started to like her. But Tucker and Emily were always around, so I never really had a chance to talk to her again."

"Did you keep up with her on her Facebook page or her website?"

"Yeah. And she had a cool website, too. I used to dream about her, meeting her, what I'd say and everything. Now, I can't even go to her sites anymore. They just don't mean anything."

"I think I understand how you feel."

Josh sounded like a typical stalker paying such close attention to Victoria.

"I better go, Mrs. Bradley. My grandma just came home and she'll want to hear all about the police coming over. Thanks for listening. I don't talk to a lot of people."

"Thanks for sharing what you know. I've hit a wall so far with finding anything. Please call me if you think of anything else. You may help me crack this case!"

"Sure. Mrs. Bradley?"

"Yes?"

"I was just wondering, if you talk to Emily again, would you tell her I'm sorry Victoria is dead? I don't think Emily has very many friends either."

"I will. That's very thoughtful of you. And I know it must be hard for you to lose her, too. Even though...."

"Yeah, even though she hardly knew who I was. It's okay. It doesn't matter. Victoria was a nice girl. It sucks that she's gone. Talk to you later."

Cecilia eyed me suspiciously. "What was that all about?"

"That was the pizza guy. He's lonely and wanted to talk. But I did find out three things. Alex Draper sells drugs, number one, and we still don't know who the other staff member was."

"And number three?"

"Number three is that Josh has a slight crush on Emily Woods. Have you found anything on Danny Pratt?"

"Nothing comes up. I'd call him a dead end. How are you going to find out who Pratt is? Aren't you exhausted, Jillian? I sure am. I can't stay awake much longer. Must be the climate here."

"This thing has me too wound up. I'll take Teddy, and you get some rest. I'll see you at breakfast in the morning. Sleep well!"

"Goodnight." She closed the door behind us.

The halls were empty. Everything was quiet. I needed my family around me. After all, that was the reason why I was here.

I quickly popped into my room to get Teddy's tote and leash, touched up my hair and makeup, and headed downstairs to search for Miguel. It seemed he was the only one brave enough to talk to me. Connie acted just plain scared when I talked to her, and those men downstairs in the boiler room had definitely been guarded.

I took the elevator down to the first floor and passed a few guests in the halls before arriving at my mom's room. I knocked softly in case she had gone to bed. There was no answer. Well then, a walk around the pool area might be a good idea. Someone might be sitting outside.

Being a widow was often lonely. Especially a widow with no children. I tried not to think about it too often, but I was made very aware of it when I saw my sister and brothers' wonderful families.

Except for Will. We were planning to hang out together until the murders happened and Stephanie showed up.

I wondered what was going on with Stephanie. Maybe I would pay my little brother a visit.

Brooke's shutters were closed for the night as I passed by her room. Daniel's room was dark as well. Probably out for dinner somewhere. I hoped Will was still here. His room was right across from the pool.

As I approached his patio, I noticed Lexis and Annika in the hot tub. They waved when they saw me and motioned for me to come over and talk to them.

"Hey, ladies. Where's your dad?"

"He's having dinner with Stephanie," said Lexis.

"And how do you feel about that?"

Annika looked at Lexis and then moved her legs back and forth in the water, pausing before she answered.

Lexis slipped into the hot tub and then faced me.

"We feel like she's a total stranger," said Annika. She had a question in her voice, not certain if it was a bad thing.

I leaned against the wall for support and tried to put myself in Stephanie's place.

"You know, she probably feels the same way about you. If you were my daughters, no power in the world would change my love for you."

"Even if you deserted them, Aunt Jillian?" asked Lexis.

"She probably loves you more because she did desert you. That's why she tried to find you again. It's why many mothers who give their children up for adoption want them returned nowadays. Maternal love."

"But what about Dad? Do you think she really loved him if she left him like that?" Annika slipped into the steaming water.

"I don't know. But the fact that she never remarried or found anyone else to be with suggests she may have always loved him. Maybe she didn't know how to let him know."

Lexis walked up the steps of the hot tub and sat on the side, dangling her feet, toenails painted dark blue, in the hot water. "Or maybe she was afraid if she did, he wouldn't take her back."

"Now you're starting to understand. Ultimately, it will be up to your dad to figure out what he wants to do. He's terribly lonely, so maybe it would be better to have Stephanie in his life than no one at all."

Annika turned her head and looked at Lexis. "She's

right, we want our dad to be happy, don't we, sis?"

Lexis shrugged, obviously still not convinced, but thinking about it.

"Of course we do. And Stephanie doesn't seem like a bad person."

"I don't think so either. In fact, she seems nice."

The girls appeared to be getting used to the idea. Perhaps it was a good sign, even if the two decided to go separate ways from their mother.

"It would take time to get used to each other, but that's true of any new situation. If your dad decided to remarry someone else, don't you think you'd have to get used to your stepmother, too? Think about it."

"That's a good point," said Lexis. "Besides, it really should be up to Dad. He's the one who would have to live with her. Right?"

"That's right. It's his life."

"So," said Annika thoughtfully, "we should let him decide what he wants to do and then support his decision."

"That's probably best, Annika."

"Well," said Lexis, "Annika's right. We'll support him either way. We love our dad and just want him to be happy."

"That's good. I'm going to see if he's in his room. If not, I'll see you all in the morning. You're leaving tomorrow, aren't you?" The thought made me sad.

"As far as we know. Dad hasn't said otherwise. But who knows? Stephanie may change our plans." She half-smiled.

"See you in the morning." I kissed their cheeks. "Love you."

"'Night, Aunt Jillian."

Will's room was dark. He would probably be home late. He and Stephanie surely had a lot to talk about. Another good sign. One never knew which direction life would take. It was good to be open to any possibility.

I walked slowly to the elevator feeling very low.

Would I ever stop missing my husband?

I thought again of hearing the fateful news of his heroic death in Vietnam, and my heart sank once more. I knew I would always think of him, and remember how much we loved each other.

Then there was Will and Stephanie. Was their love strong enough to rekindle? At least they had the real possibility. I only had the memory.

Halfway between the second and third floor, the elevator stopped abruptly. The lights flickered and went out leaving me alone in pitch-blackness. I pushed the emergency button, but got nothing. I pounded on the door and yelled for help, but no one seemed to hear.

I couldn't tell how long I was stranded. I began losing my voice from yelling so much. My hand was sore from pounding on the door. Sinking to the floor, I told myself that I would just have to wait until someone noticed that the elevator had stopped working.

How long would that be?

Just as I was about ready to give up hope, the lights flickered on and the elevator began to climb. The door opened on my floor and I stepped out, incensed that no one had come to my aid.

After reaching my room, still angry at what I'd been through, I slid the key across the lock, opened the door, and stepped inside. On the floor was a piece of paper with a note written on one side. In scrawling letters, it said, "Stay out of it."

I went into my bathroom, found my tweezers, picked up the piece of paper without disturbing any prints, and placed it in the hotel information book for safekeeping.

Who in the world would put a note like that under my door? Surely not Lee Sterling. Dr. Griffin? Maybe. Alex Draper? Seemed a little dramatic, but he might have done it. Who else then? I had to talk to Miguel.

Before getting Teddy, I took the stairs down to the lobby.

The concierge raised her eyebrows (convinced, now for sure, I was a huge nuisance) and thanked me for letting her know about the elevator getting stuck.

After marching down the hall and pressing the elevator button, the door opened normally, but I didn't get in. Not this time!

Whoever pulled the prank had to work here, that was all there was to it. That meant a staff member who had stayed in the shadows on purpose, avoiding me.

I looked up and saw Miguel wearing a tool belt walking toward me with Lucas. Miguel certainly was a versatile employee.

"Good evening, Mrs. Bradley," said Miguel. "Lucas here told me you wanted to talk to me. Lucas, would you excuse us a minute? Go see if you can get that spotlight changed out by the front door. Mr. Gonzalez wants it done right away."

Lucas nodded and got in the elevator, then pushed the button to go to the garage.

"Miguel, I was trapped in this elevator not ten minutes ago!"

"What? How did that happen?" He sounded truly surprised.

"I don't know. The car stopped halfway between the second and third floors and then the lights flickered, dimmed, and finally went out. I pounded on the doors and yelled until I couldn't anymore, and then suddenly the thing started going up again and the lights came on."

"That is very suspicious, Mrs. Bradley. I haven't been by here all evening, so I didn't see anything unusual."

"That's not the worst part. When I got back to my room, there was a note under my door that said to stay out of it. If that isn't a threat, I don't know what is!"

"Mrs. Bradley, you should tell the police, don't you think?"

"I'm not sure. All I know is, the killer must still be

here."

"It sure sounds like it. And he must be following you, or how else would he know to trap you like that? You'd better not go anywhere alone. You're in danger, and that's very bad."

His words were not encouraging. "Miguel, would you mind walking with me to my room? I'd feel better."

"Sure, Mrs. Bradley. We can take the stairs, if you wish."

"Yes, I'd rather do that. Miguel, does the staff take the stairs a lot?"

"I suppose a few do, maybe for exercise. But the housekeepers and maintenance people have to take the elevators because of the equipment they use."

"Of course."

We ascended the stairs, me going first, until we reached the third floor. The stairs were very close to the suite where Victoria was murdered, and I remembered seeing Dr. Griffin that first day taking the stairs from the third floor instead of the elevator.

"Miguel, do you remember who was working as the security guard the night Victoria was killed?"

"Let me think. It was Felix. He works on the weekends. An old guy with a nice wife and four kids. I've known him for a couple of years now, why?"

"Oh, I don't know. We're missing someone who was there that night. Looking at the roster you gave me, everyone seems to check out. Except, there wasn't a name listed for the person who helped Lucas with the tabletop. Would the security guard leave his post to do something like that?"

"I don't think so. He's supposed to be watching the hotel. He may have left. But no, I really don't think so."

"Well, someone helped Lucas that night. I must ask him."

We had arrived at my door.

"Here we are. Thank you for coming up with me. I was more angry than scared in that elevator. But, I guess I'd better take your advice and be more careful now."

"I think you'd better. Sure you're okay?"

I nodded.

"I need to go make sure Lucas took care of that light. See you tomorrow, Mrs. Bradley."

"Thanks again, Miguel."

I walked over to Cecilia's room and lightly tapped on her door.

"Where have you been?" she asked, rubbing her eyes. "Sorry, I fell asleep waiting. Teddy's crashed."

"Sorry — got a little tied up. Someone trapped me in the elevator and then slid a note under my door telling me to stay out of it."

Teddy woke up when he heard my voice.

"Really? That's crazy!"

I went to the edge of the bed where Teddy was and gently stroked his fur. "Let's just say we're on the right track. Whoever it was must work here — that's now a given."

"Or, maybe they're just handy with electrical stuff. So you'd leave out our pizza delivery guy and Alex Draper?"

"My instinct says neither one of them had enough motive to kill Victoria and her mother. I mean, Josh could have killed Victoria because he was mad about her and she didn't give him the time of day, but after I've talked to him, he doesn't seem like the type.

"Alex Draper may be a drug dealer, but there are nice drug dealers out there who see dealing as a business. Besides, why would Alex want to get rid of his buyers?"

"Maybe they wanted to quit and he didn't like the idea."

"If they wanted to quit, why did Lexis see Victoria take Ecstasy?"

"True. Good point."

"So, who does that leave?"

"Dr. Griffin, for one. He could have jimmied that elevator. I know he doesn't like me asking questions."

"What about Lee? Can you see him killing his wife and daughter?"

"In all honesty, no, I can't. Besides, what reason would he have? If Birdie and Dr. Griffin *were* having an affair, then maybe Lee would have a motive, but to kill his only child, too? It doesn't wash."

"Jillian, you look tired. Why don't you go to bed and get some rest? I'm sure you'll think more clearly when you're not so exhausted. You can call the police tomorrow about the note."

"I will. But I don't feel the least bit tired. After that elevator incident, I'm just angry that someone tried to intimidate me. Come on, Teddy, let's go to bed."

He stretched out his little paws and then his back legs. He looked at me with tired eyes and yawned.

"I'm ready whenever you are, Mistress," he seemed to convey.

"He went out about an hour ago," said Cecilia, as if reading my mind.

I took Teddy, slid my room key across the lock and opened the door. No one jumped out. The room was in order. Looked like we were safe for the moment.

After placing Teddy on his towel, he fell asleep right away. I turned off the bedroom lights.

Now for a nice hot bubble bath to wash away the cares of the day.

Soaking in the soothing hot water filled with fragrant bubbles allowed me to cast my mind over the whole time I had been here, going over each day just as it happened. It was hard to believe four days had passed so quickly. Now most of the family would be leaving in the morning. Still, there must be something I had missed. Some thread that tied all this together. But what?

"Lord," I prayed aloud, "You know what happened to

those women. Please show me the thread so we can get Chase out of jail. I trust You to guide my thoughts. Amen."

I got out of the tub, dried off and sprayed myself lavishly with my Legacy perfume. At least I would fall asleep to a pleasant aroma surrounding me instead of unpleasant thoughts about a killer on the loose.

I slid in between the cool fresh sheets and finally began to unwind. Fresh sheets…people coming into my room during the day…yes…someone came into Victoria and Birdie's rooms at some time and took their lives.

"Teddy, be on guard!"

He lifted his little head and looked at me as if he understood. He responded with a tiny growl.

I felt safer already.

18 Departures

The night was thankfully uneventful, except for waking up several times from the stressful images that haunted my mind.

The next morning, my focus was on getting presentable and taking Teddy for his morning constitutional. Teddy was wide-awake and had covered my face with dog kisses trying to rouse me out of bed.

I couldn't believe it was Wednesday already.

The very first thing I did was call Detective McKenzie and tell him about the elevator incident and the note. He told me he would make a note of it and to keep him informed of any other incidents. He said there wasn't much he could do about the attacks. Not very comforting, but at least the events had been documented for the record.

Teddy was raring to go out.

"Okay, boy, let me get dressed and we'll go downstairs for a nice walk."

Teddy yipped when he heard the word walk.

After dressing and brushing my hair and grooming Teddy, making sure he was impeccably clean, we looked presentable to go downstairs. I placed him in his tote, stuffed the leash inside, grabbed my purse, and headed for the elevator.

On second thought, I changed my mind and took the stairs. Maybe something interesting would surface. And it did. Lucas was coming up carrying a room service tray.

"Good morning, Lucas. Who's the lucky guest?" I spoke before thinking how nosy I sounded.

"Good morning, Mrs. Bradley. It's for Dr. Griffin and Mr. Sterling. Have a nice day." He hurried up the stairs.

So they were still here at the hotel. Thick as thieves, having breakfast together. Of course, they probably didn't want to be visible to curious guests.

Be visible...now, why would someone not want to be visible?

If it were me, it would be because I wasn't presentable, or maybe trying to shun a responsibility of some kind. But that was me — a law-abiding citizen.

Why would a non-law-abiding citizen not want to be visible? A crime of course, what else? Politicians try to hide facts they're ashamed of all the time, but they don't usually succeed because someone always pays someone else to dig up dirt and spread it all over the media.

I took Teddy quietly through the lobby and out the front door. The cool air enveloped me and refreshed my soul. We walked down a couple of blocks with Teddy on his leash, moving as fast as his little legs could carry him. He panted and looked up, which signaled it was time to stop.

After he finished relieving himself, he was worn out and gave me the look.

"Please pick me up and carry me," he seemed to say.

Scooping him up, I gingerly put him into his tote while instinctively glancing around, taking in my surroundings. Very few people were out this early in the morning. Only a few joggers passed by, huffing and puffing. To each his own.

Alex or Fancy didn't seem to be around, but why would they be up this early? They probably kept late hours considering the work he did dealing drugs.

I returned to the hotel and trucked up the stairs, still not over my elevator experience, and delivered Teddy to

Cecilia.

"He's all yours while I have my breakfast." I handed the tote to her. "I'll be back in a few minutes."

"Hey, take your time — I'm really in no hurry. I have a banana that will hold me. Come on, little guy."

The Caribbean Room was full of family members this morning, a sad time usually with everyone having to say goodbye. But this morning it wasn't just a sadness pervading the air, there was also a feeling of overwhelming despair.

Mom was sitting with Brooke. Greg sat at the table next to Will who looked chipper this morning and happier than I had seen him in a long time. I didn't see Lexis or Annika — they were probably sleeping in.

I waved a hello, thinking how wonderful it was that we had all been together for a few days, in spite of the terrible tragedy of Chase being incarcerated.

I looked over on the opposite side of the room and saw the other two families having breakfast — Ryan and Christina holding Paxton dressed in a cute pink shorts outfit. She looked like a big baby doll! Scott, Rachel and their two girls were standing to leave and came over to give me hugs and kisses.

"When are you all leaving?" I asked, as Mallory hugged my legs. Such a sweet little girl when she wanted to be.

"Our plane leaves at one, so we don't have to leave until 11:00 a.m.," said Rachel.

Samantha tugged at her shirt, asking for a pastry.

"Then I'll say goodbye now in case I don't see you again. Why don't you come for Christmas? I've got a big house and I'd love to have you."

Scott looked at Rachel to see what her reaction would be. He got affirmation in the form of a smile and a nod.

"That sounds wonderful, Aunt Jillian." She lifted a brow. "You want us all to come? The whole family?"

"Yes, I do. All these years I've come to your homes, and

now, I'd like to return the favor. Shall I hold you a reservation?"

Scott said, "You have my vote! Are you sure you want all of us?"

"Well, why not? There are twenty-one of us, but I'll only need to put up a few of you." Plans about where to put everyone jumbled around in my head.

Kaitlin sat within earshot of our conversation.

"'Morning, Aunt Jillian," she said as she put more Fruit Loops on Silas's tray. He sat in a high chair pulled up to the table, wearing a bear bib that said, "Grandpa's Boy."

Daniel and Paige were sitting one table over out of harm's way in case Silas decided to share his food. Kevin and Sydney were outside on the patio playing tag, but staying within eyesight of their mother.

"Did I just hear you say we're invited to your house for Christmas?" she asked with a gleam in her eye.

Kaitlin had been to my house on several occasions, and I had treated her like a queen.

"You heard correctly. Will Kenny be home from Afghanistan by then?"

"Yeah, he's due in November, hopefully, if everything goes well. We never know. I'm sorry. Silas's getting antsy. I'd better get him down and go check on the kids outside. See you at Christmas, then?"

"I'll look forward to it. Safe trip home."

Daniel motioned for me to join him after I filled my plate with a small pastry and two slices of cantaloupe.

"I need to get some coffee first."

The coffee service was set up by the door to the patio. When I glanced around I noticed Miguel gesturing as if agitated to one of the workers who was hosing off the concrete. The worker's back was to me, so I couldn't see his face. I rejoined Daniel and Paige and asked about their plans.

"Our plane leaves at eleven-thirty. We still need to pack,

but it shouldn't take too long. How about you, Jillian?"

"I'm going to stay until something gets done about Chase. Have you heard anything?"

"They took him to the county jail and booked him for murder. It's so horrible to think about, Jillian. He's waiting for an arraignment to enter a plea."

"That's what Brooke told me. And of course there's no bail for murder or a capital crime." I thought about how trapped and worried Chase must be. "At least he has a good lawyer. Is he allowed to have visitors?"

"Yeah, family, anyway. You could go see him," said Paige.

"I think I will. Have a safe trip home." I hugged Daniel and Paige and gave Silas and Kaitlin a kiss goodbye. "I'll start saying goodbye to the others."

"See you next year if not sooner, sweet sister."

Will slid over out of the booth and joined me at the table.

"'Morning, sis. How's the investigation going? Any leads?"

"A few, but they're thin." I lowered my voice. "How's Stephanie doing? I heard you were out with her last night."

Will drained his coffee and set the cup down. He took his napkin and wiped his mouth, then sighed as he continued.

"We talked for hours. She's changed, Jillian. She's still the same as far as her special quirks go, like covering her mouth when she smiles, and looking away shyly when I pay her a compliment. When I look at her, even though she and I are older now, I still see the face I fell in love with."

"So, how has she changed?" I asked.

It was obvious that Will had never stopped loving her.

"Matured? I know that sounds trite, but it's the only way I can describe her now. She's stopped running away from things she can't handle. I suppose having to make it on her own has taught her how to do that, and maybe that's what she needed, even though I would have been there for her for anything she thought she had to face.

"That's the part that hurts the most, I think, that she chose to shut me out of her life. But that was so long ago, and we still have the rest of our lives to live. I have to ask myself, do I want to go on living it alone?"

I understood what Will was saying, because without Cecilia being there for me, that would have been me.

"So now you have your answer. What about hers?"

He sighed before answering my question.

"I had a long talk with Lexis and Annika after I got home last night, that's why they're sleeping in. We stayed up until 2:00 a.m."

"How do they feel?"

"They're showing a united front. They want me to be happy, so if Stephanie decides to come home, they'll welcome her. I think they're wonderful to be so supportive."

"And Stephanie?"

"She told me she'd give me her answer after I was home for a few days. She wants me to be sure that I really want her and that this isn't just some romantic fantasy we're having because we're here in these perfect surroundings. I will tell you one thing. I asked her if she'd been with anyone else."

"What did she tell you?"

"She told me she came close once, but couldn't bring herself to do it. She didn't know if it was because of all the guilt she felt, or if it was because she still loved me."

I reached for my coffee and took a sip. It had grown cold.

Will stood. "I'll keep in touch, sis. I need to pack up and get those girls down here before breakfast ends. Take care of yourself, and we'll see you at Christmas."

"Maybe I'll see all of you then. Good luck, Will. I love you."

"Love you, too."

"Have you seen Mom this morning?"

"She's in her room packing."

"I'll go see her. Thanks."

I started to leave the table, then noticed the staff working in the kitchen looking at me. I noticed they weren't smiling as they usually did, but then, I really couldn't blame them.

I smiled at them anyway and said good morning. They simply nodded and began to clear dishes away from the tables.

I hurried upstairs to let Cecilia take a break before the breakfast service ended. I knocked lightly on her door.

"It's me," I said.

She opened the door, and Teddy bounded to greet me, stretched his paws up on my legs, and begged me to pick him up.

"Have you been a good boy while I've been gone?" I cooed.

He licked my chin, and I hugged him to my chest.

"He's had his breakfast. That was a good idea to put some of his food in my fridge."

"I thought it would be more convenient. It's nice to have that grocery store only a few blocks from here."

"Is your family ready to leave?"

"All except for Brooke and Greg, they're staying on until Chase is arraigned. I'm going over to see him sometime this afternoon. Do me a favor please and call the county jail for me and see when visiting hours are?"

"Sure."

"Oh, there's one more thing. Two, really."

"What's that?"

"Is there any way to dig a little deeper into Dr. Griffin's and Lee's backgrounds? They may be hiding something, some little thing that we're overlooking."

"Walter did a preliminary check with the police records, but maybe I can see what comes up on Google. You wouldn't believe the stuff you can find!"

"Good. Do it right away, after breakfast. You'd better get down there before it closes. I'm going to check in with my mom while you eat. Come on, Teddy, let's go see Grandmother Lovejoy."

Teddy yipped twice as if trying to tell me something.

"I know, she's not that fond of dogs, but she likes you, really!"

I picked him up and stroked him gently.

"Ready?" Cecilia asked, opening the door.

"All set. Let's go."

We headed downstairs, this time on the elevator.

I found Mom packing when I got to her room. She moved slowly as if weighted down by the family's departures. I put Teddy on the floor. He found a lovely spot underneath the chair in the corner to take a little nap. I thought he'd rather sit this one out.

"It's hard saying goodbye, isn't it?" I watched her take her clothes from the closet. She folded them lovingly over the rest of her belongings in the suitcase.

"This is the least favorite part of the reunion. I have to tell myself, that unless we say goodbye, the next reunion can't come. It helps."

"That's a good way to look at it."

"Have you found out anything to help Chase? Brooke and Greg are worried sick." She closed the suitcase and sat on the couch. I sat next to her, and patted her arm.

"I'm staying until I've done everything I know to do to find out who murdered those poor women. I keep wondering if we're looking in the wrong direction."

"What do you mean?"

"At first, I wondered, if the killer had something against Victoria or her mother that was compelling enough to kill them. Cecilia and I found out that Victoria took drugs and had an abortion, but are those reasons to kill someone?"

Mother shrugged. "Not unless she did something or was

going to do something that would ruin her suppliers somehow. And as for the abortion, I would think that would be damaging to her career if anyone found out."

I stood, walked to the window, and watched people stroll by on the boardwalk.

"I thought about that, and those are good reasons, I suppose. Since someone broke their necks, it would be hard to pin that on a female like Emily unless she had a black belt in karate or something. So that only leaves opportunity, and that, dear mother, is what I'm working on right now. Someone in this hotel had access to their rooms."

"True. Lee Sterling, that doctor, and the hotel staff come to mind."

"Correct. And that means the rest of the party goers couldn't have killed them both, because they wouldn't have access to Birdie's room, would they?"

"I don't see how. So what are you going to do next?"

"I have Cecilia trying to find out more about Lee and the doctor. I have to talk more to the staff somehow, but it's not going to be easy. They're all scared the killer will retaliate if they say anything."

"I can understand that. I hate to leave, but I'm meeting Will in the lobby. I'm riding with them to the airport. The porter should be here to get my bags any minute. Good luck, dear daughter. I'll be praying for you."

"Thanks, Mom. Safe trip home. I love you." I hugged her gently knowing the last thing she needed at her age was a bear hug.

"Come on, little guy." I gathered Teddy in my arms and headed out to the patio. "Let's go see what's going on around here."

19 Night Meeting

The hotel crowd thinned considerably, it being a Wednesday and with my family leaving. I strolled out on the patio with Teddy in my arms, scanning the private patios to see who was out and about.

Out of curiosity, I looked up to see who was on the floors above. Sitting on his patio were Lee and Doctor Griffin. I refrained from waving, but when Lee and I locked eyes, I smiled and nodded. Dr. Griffin frowned and looked at Lee sternly, as if to warn him to stay away at all costs.

At what costs, Dr. Griffin? What are you hiding that you are so afraid I'll find out?

Lee got up and went inside his room, leaving Dr. Griffin staring down at me. I smiled at him, too, in a friendly way, not wanting to appear suspicious. Perhaps eventually he would let down his guard and let me approach.

Brooke and Greg must have been in their room, since I didn't see them on their patio. They may have been with Chase. If I had a son in jail, that's where I would be.

I tried pouring myself a cup of coffee from the Caribbean Room, but it was difficult while holding Teddy. I jumped when I heard Lee's voice beside me.

"Having trouble? Here, let me help you," he said.

I couldn't help liking the warm way his voice sounded. I stepped aside and allowed him to pour my coffee.

"Sugar? Cream?" he asked.

"Black is fine, thank you, Lee. You startled me! I didn't think you'd ever want to talk to me again."

"Shall we sit? Preferably where Reed can't see us. How about over here around this corner?"

"That's fine," I felt happy to be waited on and yet apprehensive at letting him know how much I liked him. I waited for him to speak, having learned people will talk first if you listen.

"I was rude to you the other day, and I wanted to apologize. I'm sorry, will you forgive me?"

He could be so charming.

"Of course. I understand you're going through an extremely difficult time. No need for an apology, really."

"Thank you. You need to know that Reed and I go back a long way, and I felt you were on the attack. I don't understand why you think he had anything to do with what happened."

I waited until he finished, giving him plenty of time to vent.

"Lee, I'm only trying to figure out the motive. Right now, I've drawn a blank. But remember this. Someone must have really hated them to have killed them like that."

"Well, they might have just as well killed me, because I feel dead without my wife and daughter. Who could have possibly hated them so much?"

"That's what I'm trying to find out. I know this is hard for you, but is there anything you want to tell me about Dr. Griffin? Something that he wants to keep so secret that he would risk murder to keep it quiet?"

Lee looked thoughtful for a moment and then shook his head. "No, I don't know of anything like that in his past. It may be there, but he hasn't ever told me about it."

"I see." I wondered if Lee had thought of something and decided not to tell me.

"Did you know he performed an abortion on Victoria?" I waited for his reaction. His face slowly started to contort in true surprise and horror.

"What are you saying? What abortion? Where did you hear something like this?" he said in a hissing, menacing whisper.

I backed away and Teddy whimpered.

"It's okay, Teddy, Lee has just heard some bad news. You didn't know, did you? I can tell by your expression."

He covered his face with his hands, distraught.

"I'm sorry, Lee, but it could be the reason they were killed. I don't think Birdie knew about it, either. That's why it's such a mystery that she was killed, too."

"I guess it's not enough that my wife and daughter are taken from me, now I find out my grandchild is dead, too. What do I have left? I ask you, what do I have left?" He stood. "Excuse me, Jillian. I need to talk to Reed."

Lee's emotional upset caused Teddy to start shaking. I tried soothing him with comforting words. "It's okay, boy, it's okay." At least I might have shaken something up for Dr. Griffin.

Lucas walked out and began removing dishes from patio tables. I smiled and nodded, but would have preferred to be able to talk to him.

He avoided eye contact and took a circuitous route on purpose.

He must be afraid to talk to me, just like the rest of the staff.

"Come on Teddy, let's go to our room and see if Cecilia has come up with anything. We're certainly getting nowhere down here."

Just as I stood to leave, Teddy began to yip, and I was quite embarrassed at the attention he was drawing. "What is it?"

Teddy struggled to get down, so I let him, aware that something was bothering him. I had learned from previous experience to trust these little dogs' instincts — he could be on to something.

I quickly attached his leash and let him go.

Teddy led me, yipping and pulling on his leash toward the boardwalk gate, dragging me along.

I swiped my key across the lock to gain access and opened the gate, searching for what was bothering him. He continued pulling me as fast as his little legs could carry him, until I saw where he was headed.

Fancy pulled her master as well, trying to reach Teddy as fast as Teddy was pulling me along trying to reach her. Talk about a dog's scent ability!

I was almost out of breath by the time I reached Alex. I had to laugh at our situation. He thought it was funny, too, I could tell.

"Hey, slow down, Fancy, I see them!" he told her.

We finally reached each other and found a bench to sit on to catch our breath.

"I don't know what got into her," he said. "She just took off running all of a sudden. I barely got hold of her leash."

"Same thing with Teddy. Look at them!"

Teddy and Fancy were sitting side by side with both their tongues hanging out of their mouths, panting from the run. "They must have sensed we needed to find each other," I said, hoping I could learn something from this enigmatic young man.

"How's your nephew doing?" he asked.

"Not good. They still think he did it. And why wouldn't they? He had an argument with Victoria that everyone witnessed the night before, he's a Marine with killing skills, and was at the party. The nail in the coffin, though, was that he was the one to find her. If I were Detective McKenzie, I'd have arrested him, too."

"I'm sorry," he said lamely.

"Are you, Alex? Then help me find out who did this."

"What do you want me to do, confess? I didn't do it!" He was getting more agitated and lashed out. "Why would I kill Victoria, let alone her mother, for crying out loud? Stop and think about it!"

I continued to press on, unruffled by his defensiveness.

"Let's say you were supplying drugs through Dr. Griffin."

"Dr. Griffin? Him? No way. Why would I deal him in? Besides, I think he's a scumbag."

"Why would you say that?"

"Well, for one thing he was always on the make for Birdie. And another thing, I know he was blackmailing someone."

"Care to tell me who?"

"I've said enough, Mrs. Bradley."

"You know, Alex, you're heading for disaster with what you're doing. Nothing good is going to come from it, you must realize that."

"Thanks for your concern, but I can handle myself. Besides, it's too late to get out. Once you're in, you're in. Sorry, I've got an appointment. I'll see you around. Come on, Fancy, mission accomplished."

Fancy followed reluctantly. Teddy watched her until they were out of sight.

I sat and thought about what Alex had told me. I was right about one thing: Dr. Griffin was on the make for Birdie. He was not a gentleman, for sure. Blackmail?

Maybe it was a patient, but how would Alex know? Unless he saw it firsthand. Victoria? Birdie? Lee? Not Lee, why would he protect him in that case?

Nothing made sense.

Walking home slowly, holding a tuckered out little dog, Teddy and I reached the hotel and went through the lobby. I realized my family had left by now. I felt sad. I was too tired to walk up the stairs, so I took the elevator closest to the lobby instead of the one at the far end of the hall closest to my room, just in case.

I made sure the desk clerk saw me enter and then pushed the button for the third floor. There was a stop on the

second floor, where one of the staff joined me. He selected
the ground floor and looked at the ceiling. I noticed his
nameplate said Zach Ramirez, but before I could say a
word, I reached the third floor and stepped off, taking a last
look at him before the door closed. He was looking at me
with a strange expression in his eyes. An alarm went off in
my head, trying to think what it was that I needed to
remember! Maybe I was inventing it, but I felt he knew
something.

It was lunchtime, and I was famished after all that
running. I wondered if Cecilia had ordered any food.

I knocked quickly on her door. She let me in, happy to
see me.

"Have you ordered lunch yet?" I asked, putting Teddy in
the bathroom where he lapped thirstily until the water dish
was almost completely empty.

"Yes, I did. Sorry, I couldn't wait. How about you?"

"No, Teddy and I have been on a little excursion down
on the boardwalk."

"Really? What happened?"

"Well, I said goodbye to everyone except for Brooke and
Greg because they're staying on. I suppose I should also
tell you that I saw Lee and Dr. Griffin sitting on their
balcony. When Lee saw me, he came down right away and
helped me get my coffee. He also apologized for being so
off putting yesterday."

"Wow! That was nice of him."

"However, I brought up Dr. Griffin again and asked Lee
if he knew about Victoria's abortion."

"And did he?"

"No. He took it quite badly. After that, he excused
himself and went to talk to Griffin. Teddy dragged me
down the boardwalk to find Fancy, who was trying to find
him. I guess it was a dog instinct-scent thing. Anyway, I
hooked up with Alex again and did some more probing. I
found out Alex thinks our dear doctor is a blackmailer."

"No way!"

"Oh, yes, way. And get this. I was right about him trying to put the make on Birdie."

"What about the blackmail? Did Alex tell you who the doctor is blackmailing?"

"Unfortunately, no. He wouldn't tell me. But I assume he witnessed it, or knows someone who did, so it might be material evidence. And that's what we need. Let me order up some lunch first, and we'll talk some more."

Ordering pizza seemed like a good way to talk to Josh again *if* he was working. Pizza was not one of my favorites, but it might be worth it if it gave me a chance to question him.

Hmm.

Nothing on the menu looked healthy. No, wait. The chicken and vegetable one looked okay — not too fattening.

I placed the order and plopped down in Cecilia's chair.

Josh brought my pizza to the room, as requested, still wearing the long baggy shorts ensemble. I signed the bill and invited him to chat for a moment.

"Okay," he said, "but I have to do some more deliveries. What's going on?"

"Nothing. That's the problem. I just felt like some of your great pizza," I fibbed.

Lord, forgive me.

"Oh, I talked to Emily last night," he said, as if suddenly remembering.

"Good for you! I haven't talked to her."

"Yeah, I decided to tell her myself how sorry I was about Victoria and her mom. She seemed happy to hear from me, which is very cool.

"You know, Emily is shy, kind of like me. She said I could come over sometime if I wanted, so I think I might get her to like me. I've never had a girlfriend because I'm shy. I don't think Emily's ever had a boyfriend, either. That makes us kind of even, huh?"

"That's great, Josh! She's going to be okay with Dr. Griffin and everything?"

"Him?" Josh asked with a sudden alertness. "That guy's no good. Emily is scared of him."

"What for? Has he ever threatened her?"

"It's not like that," he said. "I think that guy's got something over the Sterling's, well, Victoria's dad, anyway."

"What did she say? This is interesting, Josh."

Just then, Josh's pager beeped and he started to rush off.

"Sorry, I have to go, see you later."

Cecilia and I just looked at one another as I opened the pizza box and took out a slice.

She handed me a plate to put it on and shrugged.

Chase was happy I had come to visit him. He looked gaunt and worried — not the same person I had seen leaving the hotel a few days ago.

Had it only been three days since he was carried off to jail?

I did my best to let him know we were doing everything we could to get him released. He thanked me, but I could tell by the way he shuffled out of the room, with his shoulders drooping, that he was extremely discouraged.

After the visit I returned to the hotel and went upstairs to my room. I was at my lowest point in this affair, feeling like I had gotten nowhere in the past three days.

I knocked on Cecilia's door to get Teddy. She was on the phone with Walter but ushered me in. I motioned I would just get Teddy to give her some privacy.

My bed looked so inviting I surrendered to a nap. Teddy seemed to appreciate one, too, as I put him on his towel at the foot of my bed. I crashed, my thoughts swirling until I finally yielded to sleep and went under for two blissful hours.

When my eyes popped open, I looked at the clock and saw that it was almost six o'clock. I got up, shook my head and stretched my arms overhead in an effort to wake up fully.

Sweet little Teddy stretched, too. He cocked his head and looked at me as if to say, "We haven't played together today."

"Oh, I know precious pup, but we did have a walk and rendezvous with Alex and Fancy. Doesn't that count for something?"

Teddy merely whimpered, causing a slight shiver of foreboding to run down my spine.

I checked with Brooke and Greg about dinner plans. They were having room service tonight and turning in early...exhausted from the past few days.

Cecilia knocked on my door and stepped inside. She told me all about how Walter was doing, how much he missed her (and me, too, she said).

Such a fine young man she had married. I would always feel like I had a special place in their lives, since I was the one who encouraged her to let him know how she felt about him, after which he proposed.

Walter also credited me for being the one to inspire him to get into police work after I helped solve a string of homicides in Half Moon Bay where he was working.

Of course, Cecilia was the one who spotted Teddy's kidnapper in that case, too, so we had been inextricably connected ever since.

"Do you feel like going out for dinner, Cecilia? We could find somewhere to eat outside so Teddy could go with us."

"You know, I'd just as soon order in and go to bed early — there's a movie on that I want to watch."

"That sounds good to me, too. Well, I'll see you tomorrow then. Thanks for taking such good care of Teddy for me today."

"He's a little doll. And he minds! You've done a good job training him."

"Why, thank you. Did you hear that, Teddy? You got a good report from your sitter."

He raised his ears, cocked his head and then yipped, letting me know it was time for me to feed him.

After I set out Teddy's supper of roast beef, veggies, brown rice, fruit, a sprinkle of cheese and small cups of milk and fresh water, room service arrived with my Grilled Chicken Caesar Salad.

I signed the bill, and noted a different staff member making the delivery. I closed the door and started to shut down for the evening. I took a final look at my e-mails, logged off my computer, and then switched on the TV to find some local news.

There was nothing on the Sterling cases, so I found a movie to watch while I ate my salad in silence. I notified room service that my tray was ready to pick up anytime.

The hour grew late. Room service didn't come until almost nine o'clock, which I found strange. Finally, there was a knock and a man said, "Room Service." I opened the door, and standing there was Miguel.

"I've come for the tray," he said.

"Please come in. I didn't know you worked in housekeeping, too," I said.

"Actually, I don't. I need to speak with you. I told Connie I would come get the tray."

"Why, of course. Sit down, Miguel. What's this all about?"

He sat at the desk, I put Teddy on the bed, and then I sat in the chair by the bed. Miguel looked miserable and under extreme stress.

"Where do I begin?" he said. He handed me a large manila envelope marked with 'Police' on the front. "This is my son's signed confession for the police."

Confession? I was shocked!

I reached out slowly to take the envelope, my mind racing with all the implications.

"Signed confession? You mean Zach killed those women?"

"It's not his fault, Mrs. Bradley. He did it out of love for my wife and me. He did it for our little girl, Caroline."

"I think you'd better tell me the whole story. I simply can't imagine your son doing such a heinous thing! You mean he was the one who scared me in the elevator and put that note under my door?"

"I'm sorry, but yes, he did that, too. Everything is in there," he said, pointing to the envelope. "He has asked me to let you read it first, so you'll understand that he's sorry your nephew was jailed because of what he did."

"Excuse me a moment." I went into the bathroom and found a pair of tweezers in my makeup bag. Using them carefully, I pulled the confession out of the envelope. That way, Zach's prints wouldn't be disturbed. I took a look at the first page of the confession, a story really, simply entitled, "The Truth about Monday Night."

"He thought if you read it first, when he turns himself in, you might be willing to be there when he does. I told him his mother and I would be there, too. He's a good boy, Mrs. Bradley. He's never been any trouble for us. We were so proud of him...until this happened.

"Now he has brought shame on himself and to our family. My wife and I are very afraid for what will happen to him."

I read their son's confession and placed it in the envelope. "I'm so sorry, Miguel. I will go down to the jail with you and your wife. I'll try and talk to Detective

McKenzie and see what I can do to help him."

"Oh, thank you, Mrs. Bradley. Thank you, so much!"

"I noticed you talking to someone this morning by the pool. Was that Zach with you?"

"Yes. Something deep inside of my spirit told me it was Zach. He was coming home late to avoid my wife and me. I confronted him about staying out so late these past few nights. That's when he told me he needed to talk.

"We sat in my car on my break and he told me what he did. We're very strong Catholics, Mrs. Bradley. We believe that if we confess our sins, God will forgive us. Deep down inside, Zach believes this, too. That's the reason he gave me the confession to give to the police.

"But I couldn't bring myself to be the one to do it. That's why I'm giving it to you. I need to get back to work, now. I'm very sorry about your nephew being wrongly accused. I hope this will free him."

"Thank you. I hope it will, too."

"I'll see you tomorrow morning."

With his head hung down in utter discouragement, Miguel walked out of the room.

I'm sure he felt hopeless for his son as he closed the door behind him.

20 Another Homicide

I couldn't move after I finished reading Zach's account of the murders. I knew the police would believe his story — it fit in perfectly with the events I remembered over the past few days.

There was the arrival of the Sterling entourage on Saturday. I remembered Zach and another worker staring at the group, holding some equipment, waiting for the elevator. That was when Zach first recognized Lee from his name at the trial as being the man who ran over his little sister Caroline twelve years earlier. Zach had overheard the desk clerk, Angelina, telling the Sterling's they would be staying in the penthouse suite.

As they waited for the elevator, Zach heard Victoria telling Emily they would be throwing a party there Monday night, since her dad would be away on business.

That was when Zach began formulating his plan to get revenge for all the misery Lee Sterling had brought on Zach's family, particularly on his mother who was never the same after Caroline's death.

Zach explained that simply to kill Lee would only punish his wife and daughter who had nothing to do with Caroline's death. At first, Zach believed that if he killed Victoria, it would be enough to punish Lee. An eye for an eye.

Lee had been acquitted of the felony, Zach wrote,

because the jury had identified too closely with him, thinking it could have happened to them just as easily. The case was ruled accidental.

Lee walked away, a free man. Zach later learned that Lee had bribed a judge to conduct the trial in his favor, which made Zach hate Lee all the more.

Zach's family was poor. They had no means to do anything about justice for Caroline's death, until Lee Sterling walked into the hotel last Saturday.

I thought about the scripture that says, 'Vengeance is mine, I will repay, says the Lord.' Unfortunately, now Zach would pay with his own life, probably by spending the rest of it in prison once he turned himself in for committing a premeditated murder.

What a tragedy and loss for Miguel and his wife —they would lose their only other child, and for what?

I knew Zach believed what he did was justified, but I didn't think he understood the price he must pay, nor the pain it would cause his parents.

I decided I would offer to pay for Zach's lawyer. Perhaps he could enter a plea of temporary insanity or justifiable homicide. Maybe he could get a reduced sentence, which would be better than a life sentence or the death penalty. I would call Walter in the morning to find out who he would recommend.

"Lord, have mercy on Zach," I whispered.

I had witnessed the front desk receiving a call from Birdie complaining about a light that wasn't working. I had even watched as Zach was asked to do the repair, thereby giving him access to her room.

He wrote that he decided at that time to kill Birdie as well, because after Caroline's death, his mother was only an empty shell of what she once was. He wanted Lee to feel that emptiness, that loss of not only a daughter, but also a wife.

I learned from Miguel that Zach was accepted into the

Marines after high school. He had been an exemplary recruit. It must have been a perfect outlet for his anger at what had happened to his family.

I vaguely remembered Miguel telling me about Zach joining the last time we were here. The skills Zach learned had equipped him to kill silently and quickly by twisting his victim's necks, which was the method he had used on Victoria and Birdie.

On Monday night, Zach had been on call, not scheduled to work. He had made sure no one would have a record of seeing him that day. He waited until late.

After carefully avoiding the security camera checkpoints, Zach knocked on Victoria's door, saying he was from housekeeping. Someone let him in. Seeing he was in uniform, they probably thought nothing of it.

Zach began clearing trash from the bar. He said no one even noticed since the music was loud and everyone was drunk, dancing, or passed out.

He drugged the opened bottles of liquor, making sure everyone would be unconscious when he returned. After hiding in the staircase where he could see the sober guests leave, Zach slipped on a pair of plastic gloves.

Carrying two clean towels he had hidden on the stairs in case anyone saw him, he knocked quietly, making sure everyone would be unconscious. Since no one answered, he knew it was safe.

Using his passkey, Zach entered the suite at 3:00 a.m. He stepped over Emily and Chase passed out in the living room, went into Victoria's room and broke her neck.

Avoiding the security cameras once again, he slipped silently into Birdie's room, knowing Lee was away, and killed her, too. He went down the stairs to avoid being seen, took off his uniform shirt and left through a back door, disposing of the plastic gloves in a trash can before getting into his car parked a block away.

With Chase jailed for the crimes, Zach felt in the clear,

but he couldn't get past Miguel. They were too close. Miguel loved his son with all his heart. Convincing him to write the confession was probably the hardest thing he ever had to do, besides burying Caroline.

It was over…it was late.

I must get some sleep.

Tomorrow would be here in a few hours. I had so many people to call — Brooke and Greg, Cecilia, Detective McKenzie….

I took a quick bath, no bubbles tonight and no spritz of perfume (I was simply too tired). I crawled into bed.

Teddy lifted his little head, half asleep, but plopped it down again, satisfied I was safe and sound for the night as we both fell asleep.

The next morning I dressed, fed Teddy and made my calls. Cecilia was full of questions, but I told her I would fill her in after I went down to meet with Detective McKenzie.

I dropped Teddy off with her and grabbed a little breakfast with Brooke and Greg in the Caribbean Room. They came with me, anxious to get Chase out of jail.

When we arrived, Miguel was waiting, talking with Detective McKenzie. Miguel looked like he had aged since last night. The poor man. Detective McKenzie answered a call while we waited.

"When?" The detective asked. "I see. Thanks." He hung up and turned to face us. "I'm sorry, but we've just had another homicide down on the boardwalk. I told them I'd be down as soon as I can. Now, what's this meeting all about? You say you have a confession for the Sterling murders?" He looked doubtful.

I handed him the envelope. I explained that I used tweezers so I wouldn't contaminate the prints. He thanked me but looked at me sarcastically.

It didn't matter.

"Please have a seat, everyone," he said. After slipping on some plastic gloves, he took the confession out of the envelope and began to read. Halfway through, he picked up his phone and called for an APB on Zach Ramirez.

"He's turning himself in this morning, Detective," I told him.

"Are you sure about that?"

"Unless...." My mind suddenly turned to the homicide call. I felt a wave of nausea. "I think you need to check out that call right now."

Could it be Zach? Suicide?

Miguel must have sensed what I was thinking because he pleaded with the detective as well.

"Okay, I'm going." McKenzie finally agreed.

"Brooke, you and Greg wait here with Miguel in case Zach comes in. I'll go with Detective McKenzie." I looked at him and whispered, "Just in case you need someone to make an identification."

"Come on then. Let's go."

A crowd formed around the spot where the victim had been found. Police restrained the onlookers as Detective McKenzie and I approached the scene. There, huddled over a body covered with newspaper, stood Fancy, forlorn... whimpering.

"Detective, I know this dog. Won't you please let me see if I can get her to come to me?"

He reluctantly agreed.

"Here, Fancy. Come here, girl," I gently coaxed, walking slowly toward her. "It's your friend, Jillian. Come here, girl, it's going to be all right, it's going to be all right," I soothed. I bent down slowly. When I reached her, I lowered my hand for her to smell me. She sniffed and didn't back away. "Good girl." I reached out, taking hold of her collar. I petted her gently, consoling her the best I could.

"Well, look at you, would ya," he said. "You know this dog you say?"

"Her name is Fancy, and I believe you'll find her owner under those newspapers." More and more of the investigative team arrived and began taking pictures.

Fancy began shaking, poor dog. My heart went out to her.

"Why don't you and the dog wait in the car until I get some information here, okay?" He sounded a little more agreeable.

"Certainly. Come on Fancy — let's go sit in the car." She followed me at first, but then turned and ran away as fast as she could, scared and confused without her master. I did my best to get an officer to chase her, but no one cared. Fancy disappeared down the boardwalk and ran into a nearby neighborhood until she was out of sight.

Lord, please protect Fancy.

Detective McKenzie finally wrapped up the scene with his team, then got into the car where I patiently waited. He looked at me for a moment and shook his head.

"So, mind telling me who our victim is? There's no ID on him anywhere. Could have been a robbery."

"I'll tell you if you tell me how he was killed."

"I could arrest you for obstructing justice."

"Or you could save a lot of time by knowing his name."

He paused for a moment and acquiesced. "Okay, okay, but I never told you. Deal?"

"Deal. You first."

"He was stabbed. There. What's his name?"

"Where was he stabbed?" I asked.

"Doggone it, Mrs. Bradley," he said angrily, "why does it matter to you, anyway?"

"I'm sorry, I can't help it. It's my nature to be curious. Where was he stabbed?"

Detective McKenzie ran his hand over his hair in futility.

"He was stabbed in the neck. It severed his spinal cord. Satisfied?"

"Thank you. His name was Alex Draper."

"Friend of yours?"

"In a way. Our dogs met a couple of days ago...."

"Your dogs met?" He looked at me in disbelief.

"Yes, and we made small talk until...."

"Until...."

"Until my dog, Teddy, and Fancy, Alex's dog, felt compelled to see each other again. They were the ones who brought Alex and me together for a meeting." (I knew I sounded crazy trying to explain the story, but it was the truth!)

"Let's get back to the station, ma'am. I need some coffee."

"That sounds lovely!"

He rolled his eyes and started the car. I looked out the rear view window where I watched Alex's body being placed in a black bag, zipped up and placed on a gurney, ready to be loaded into an SUV and taken to the morgue.

What happened, Alex?

21 Disappearance

After we returned to the station, Miguel, Brooke and Greg met us as we entered the building. Zach was not with them.

"No sign of Zach?" I asked Miguel. He sadly shook his head and looked down.

"You all wait in my office," said Detective McKenzie, "while I get some coffee. Anyone want any?"

Brooke, Greg and Miguel shook their heads.

"I do, please, black." I said.

He simply looked at me, and then walked down the hall to the kitchen.

Miguel was in agony.

"It…it wasn't…."

"No, Miguel, it wasn't Zach. I'm sure he'll be here soon."

Returning with the coffee, Detective McKenzie handed a cup to me, pulled his chair out from his desk and plopped down. He motioned for all of us to sit and took a long sip of his coffee as he did so.

For a moment, I tried to imagine where we would be without coffee to help us gather strength for our day. It was not a pleasant thought.

The detective sat his coffee on his desk. He looked at Miguel first.

"Now, Mr. Ramirez, tell me about your son."

After an hour of questioning Miguel, I interrupted the conversation.

"Excuse me, but don't you have what you need to let Chase go? He didn't kill those women — Zach's confession proves it."

"Just keep calm, Mrs. Bradley. Excuse us, won't you?" he said to the others. "Why don't you all wait outside or go get a drink of water. I need to tell the lady something."

The three of them stood, and acted glad to be able to move about under all the stress of the interrogation.

Detective McKenzie closed the door, turned, and smiled very briefly.

"It's going to be okay. This confession proves Zach did it, by the way. We kept a piece of crucial evidence from Chase and grilled him on it. He never cracked."

"Which part do you mean?"

"Zach described taking a lipstick from Victoria's bathroom after he killed her and drawing a letter 'C' on the mirror. The 'C' was for Caroline, he said. He drew one on Birdie's mirror, too."

"And you thought that 'C' was put there by Chase, didn't you?"

"Yes, that's correct. But we never told him about it and, like I said before, he never mentioned it."

"Because he didn't see it. He took one look at Victoria, saw that she was dead and called the police immediately."

"Correct again. It wasn't written very large, which we found interesting. Usually when a killer leaves a message like that, it's larger than life. But this one was only about four inches high, indicating it was written by someone in control, unlike someone, say for instance, who was high on something."

"And Chase could have easily overlooked it. Sir, what's going to happen to Zach? He must have gone insane when he saw that family waltz into the hotel."

"Maybe he did. You never know how a jury is going to react. But first, we have to bring him in. Any idea where he is, ma'am?"

"No idea. As far as I knew, he was turning himself in this morning."

There was a look between us both thinking the same thought. *He's fleeing the country. Mexico?*

But neither of us said anything.

I continued to look with determination at the detective to get Chase released.

Finally, he reacted.

"I'll make the call now. Tell his parents they can pick him up."

"I think you should deliver him to the hotel where you found him, don't you, Detective?"

It was inconsiderate to expect Brooke and Greg to have to navigate somewhere in a strange city after all they'd been through.

"I'll make the arrangements."

"Thank you. That's very kind. Now, I'm going to the hotel if you've finished with me."

"Sure. I think that will be all for now. I'm kind of glad you came down. That tip on Alex Draper may pan out."

"You know, you may want to question a Dr. Reed Griffin on that one. He's a guest at the hotel. I think you'll find an interesting connection if you dig deep enough. Goodbye, Detective."

I turned to leave, opened the door and kept walking before he could call me.

I was concerned about Miguel. When I came into the hall, Brooke and Greg were waiting for the cab to arrive so they could go and get their son. I silently thanked God for

Chase's release.

Miguel sat by himself on a bench focusing on his hands as they lay folded in his lap. He looked up when I approached.

"He's not coming, is he, Mrs. Bradley?"

I shook my head. "It doesn't look like it. Miguel, if I were to hire a good lawyer...."

"Oh, no, thank you, but Zach wouldn't have a chance. He killed those women, Mrs. Bradley. Killed them! He must pay, whether it's in this life or the next."

"But, if he had a good lawyer, perhaps he could get a reduced sentence by a temporary insanity plea. It's been done. I'm more than willing to pay."

"Thank you, Mrs. Bradley, but I wouldn't ask you to do that. Zach will have to choose what he will do, but knowing him, I don't think he would want to go through a trial, not after what our family went through with Caroline and that man."

"You mean Lee Sterling?"

"Yes. You've been very kind to me. I'm truly grateful for all you've done to try and help us, but I think it's best for everyone to end our talk now."

"I understand. Well, if things change, I'm still willing to help, okay?" I took a card from my purse and handed it to him. "Here, take this just in case. And good luck to you both. Please tell your wife that I will pray for your family."

"That is very kind, I will tell her. Goodbye, Mrs. Bradley. Perhaps I'll see you next year."

"I hope so, Miguel. I hope so."

Miguel walked, forlorn, out the front door.

I silently prayed for God to protect Zach and give his family strength and courage to face the days ahead.

I caught a cab to the hotel. I felt burdened for Miguel but relieved for Chase and my family. I couldn't wait to tell everyone the good news. I wondered about Fancy and hoped that someone would give her a good home. If she hadn't run away, I might have found some good-hearted soul to take her in. Funny the way life goes.

The cab dropped me off in front of the hotel. I went inside through the lobby where new guests were checking in for the weekend. There were couples, families with children racing around looking at the bronze cranes, and a few who looked like business people.

I walked past the gift shop and peeked at the display to see if anything else caught my eye before I had to leave and go home. But I had lost my appetite for shopping after all that had happened.

As I turned into the Caribbean Room to get a cup of coffee, I looked out on the patio and saw a few people sitting outside. No one I knew. I scanned the pool out of habit, looking for a familiar face but I didn't see one.

The reunion had finally ended.

Time to go home, write my column, tend the garden, have dinner with friends...enter into my routine again. I missed my family already.

Cecilia was happy to see me again and wanted to hear all about what happened at the station. I asked her to book a flight home first of all. She complied at once. I was so fortunate to have her for my assistant. She was one in a million.

I put my coffee on the end table, gathered Teddy on my lap and gave him several kisses on his sweet little head. I took a sip of my coffee and sighed from the intensity of the morning's events.

"Jillian, you must tell me what happened. I'm dying to know!"

I recounted Zach's confession, the release of Chase — the sympathy I felt for Miguel's family. My cell phone rang and I excused myself to answer it.

"Jillian, it's Lee." I was surprised at first to hear from him, but I was glad he was calling.

"I suppose Detective McKenzie has told you the news."

"I just talked to him. I suppose I feel relieved to know who did it, but when I heard his motive, I feel even worse than not knowing. Can you understand?"

"Yes, I can. But you can feel good about my nephew going free. Think about how you'd feel knowing he would be imprisoned for life or given the death penalty for something he didn't do."

"You're right. I'll think about that. Jillian, I'd like to see you before you leave."

"I'd like that. I'll call you after Cecilia books our flight home. Would that be okay?"

"Sure. I'm leaving today, too."

"What about Dr. Griffin?"

"Funny you should ask. He's down at the police station having a conversation with Detective McKenzie right now."

"I see."

"You don't sound surprised. Anyway, what about lunch?"

"Well, I never did get those fish tacos at Taco Surf."

"Taco Surf it is. Call me when you know your flight."

"Will do." After we hung up, my heart skipped a beat. Cecilia just looked at me with that knowing look.

"Jillian?"

"Do you have our flights booked?" I changed the subject.

Lee and I walked down the street and crossed over at the corner to Taco Surf. Dimly lit, with surfboards hanging from the ceiling, the taqueria was crowded as usual with a long line of customers.

I found a small table by the window and waited for Lee

to bring our food. I found him attractive and loved having the company, but I wondered if it was the mystery connected to Dr. Griffin that had *kept* me attracted. After all, Lee was a murderer for all intents and purposes since he ran down poor little Caroline. The memory would always be with him, if he had any conscience at all.

The fish tacos, rice and beans were just as delicious as I remembered them from year to year. We ate in silence, savoring the food. I wiped my mouth daintily with my napkin and pushed my plate away.

He did the same.

"So, tell me about Dr. Griffin. I know he has some kind of hold over you. I think Alex Draper was killed because he was blackmailing your friend."

Lee looked at me in astonishment and then relaxed his shoulders as if in defeat.

"It doesn't matter anymore. You're very perceptive, Jillian. I don't know how you do it, except you're very intelligent and observant."

"And I listen, Lee. At first, Alex tried to get me to think that Dr. Griffin was blackmailing you. But after he was killed, I realized it was the other way around, wasn't it?"

"Yeah. To tell you the truth I really don't care anymore. You see, after I had that DUI, my lawyer told me I could expunge it from my records. It never showed up after that, and I felt free to conduct business as usual. I put the whole thing past me. The only ones who knew, besides Birdie and the little girl's family, was Dr. Griffin."

"Her name was Caroline, Lee. She was only five years old."

"I know, I know. I used to see her in my dreams all the time after it happened. I was so drunk that I don't even remember what I was doing in that neighborhood. I'm sorry it happened. I was a different man then."

"I apologize — it's not my place to make you feel bad."

"Anyway, you're half right. Reed was blackmailing me.

Somehow, Alex found out about it and started blackmailing him. I guess he wanted a cut of the money I was paying. Anyway, the police came and picked Reed up for questioning. What happened, anyway?"

"Alex Draper was murdered last night by someone who severed his spinal cord. I believe Dr. Griffin killed him. He'd know just where to strike."

"Jillian, no!" Lee slumped in his chair. "They'll want to question me, won't they? Then everything will come out again."

"You're his best friend," I said sarcastically.

I decided under the circumstances, our relationship could never be and decided to end it, whatever it was. I felt if we continued, we would always be reminded of the grim realities of all the deaths surrounding him.

I said goodbye, wished him luck and stood.

He sat there, lost in thought.

I left quietly without a word.

EPILOGUE

Two days after arriving home in Clover Hills, I got the news that Cecilia and Walter were expecting. I suspected so at the reunion with all her nausea and extra tiredness.

Such wonderful news. I almost felt like I was going to be a grandma! The baby was due in January. How exciting for them! Even though they were both surprised they would be parents so soon after they were married, they were still very happy with the news.

I poured myself a cup of nice hot tea and stirred in three lumps of sugar, quite a lot, I knew, but that was how I liked my tea.

"Come on, Teddy. Let's go into the conservatory and sit awhile — I need a break." Teddy had been lying lazily on the sofa, recuperating from his trip to Pacific Beach. It was quite an adventure for the little fella. I wondered about Fancy. Would she find a new owner? Was she roaming the streets, hungry?

Teddy cocked his head and looked at me, as if reading my thoughts.

"You're one lucky little dog, did you know that? Poor Fancy might be homeless and hungry right now."

At the mention of Fancy's name, he yipped and jumped down from the sofa to follow me into the conservatory.

We sat on my rattan settee, and I drank my tea.

Just as I began to practice Teddy's commands, I got a call from Will. I hoped it was good news about Stephanie.

Teddy went to the conservatory door and scratched to be let out. I opened the door for him and he rushed outside, his little paws barely touching the ground.

"Will, it's good to hear from you."

"I had to call and see if you got home okay. Mom called everyone to tell us about Chase. Jillian, you're something else. My hat's off to you, sister."

"Well, thank you. I'm just glad we got Chase off the hook. When I say we, I must give God the credit for guiding my thoughts, it wasn't all me."

"That's right. But you still did all the leg work." He paused.

I knew there was another reason he was calling.

"How are you doing?" I asked.

"I'm doing fine, really. Stephanie is back in the picture."

"She is? Is this a good thing?"

"I think it is. We're going to take it slow at first, but after she came to see us, we voted to keep her. The girls have been wonderful, Jillian. I think it's because of that talk they told me they had with you at the hot tub one night."

"I'm glad I was able to help. You all will have adjustments to make. It won't be easy, but at least your life will be interesting."

"That's for sure!"

"I want you to know that I have a great deal of respect for your decision to get together again. It proves you really understand the meaning of love. I'm happy for all of you. Now, I insist you come for Christmas. Please tell Stephanie for me."

"Don't worry. We'll look forward to it. Jillian, I've got to run. I have an appointment in just a few minutes. Good to talk with you. I love you."

"I love you, too."

Christmas. Let's see now, with everyone coming I'd better check on those sheets upstairs, they might need replacing...and where am I going to put everyone?

I began to make a list.

THE END

If you enjoyed
PACIFIC BEACH,
please leave a review on your favorite reading site.

Thank you!

Go Jillian and Teddy!

Also by Nancy Jill Thames

MURDER IN HALF MOON BAY
Book 1

THE GHOST ORCHID MURDER
Book 2

FROM THE CLUTCHES OF EVIL
Book 3

THE MARK OF EDEN
Book 4

WAITING FOR SANTA
Book 6

THE RUBY OF SIAM
Book 7

THE LONG TRIP HOME
Book 8

MURDER AT MIRROR LAKE
Book 9

MURDER AT THE EMPRESS HOTEL
Book 10

MUSEUMS CAN BE MURDER
Book 11

*THE JILLIAN BRADLEY
SHORT STORY COLLECTION*

ABOUT THE AUTHOR

Nancy Jill Thames was born to write mysteries. From her early days as the neighborhood storyteller to the Amazon Author Watch Bestseller List, she has always had a vivid imagination and loves to solve problems – perfect for plotting whodunits. In 2010, Nancy Jill published her first mystery *Murder in Half Moon Bay*, introducing her well-loved protagonist Jillian Bradley, and clue-sniffing Yorkie, "Teddy."

When she isn't plotting Jillian's next perilous adventure, Nancy Jill travels between Texas, California, and Georgia finding new ways to spoil her grandchildren, playing classical favorites on her baby grand, or having afternoon tea with friends.

She lives with her husband in Texas and is a member of American Christian Fiction Writers.

To learn more about Nancy Jill, visit
http://www.nancyjillthames.com
or contact her at jillthames@gmail.com.

Made in the USA
San Bernardino, CA
16 August 2018